Jump to the Top

Patricia Leitch started riding when a friend persuaded her to go on a pony trekking holiday – and by the following summer she had her own Highland pony, Kirsty. She wrote her first book shortly after this and writing is now her full-time occupation, but she has also done all sorts of different jobs, including being a riding-school instructor, groom, teacher and librarian. She lives in Renfrewshire, Scotland, with a bearded collie called Meg.

Other pony books in Armada by Patricia Leitch

A Horse for the Holidays
The Horse from Black Loch
Dream of Fair Horses

'Jinny at Finmory' series

For Love of a Horse
A Devil to Ride
The Summer Riders
Night of the Red Horse
Gallop to the Hills
Horse in a Million

More of Patricia Leitch's books will be published in Armada

JUMP
TO THE TOP

Patricia Leitch

Armada

Jump to the Top was first published under the title
Jacky Jumps to the Top in hardback in 1973 by
William Collins Sons & Co. Ltd., London and Glasgow.
First published in Armada in the U.K. in 1981 by
Fontana Paperbacks,
14 St. James's Place, London SW1A 1PS.

© William Collins Sons & Co. Ltd., 1972

Printed in Great Britain by
Love & Malcomson Ltd., Brighton Road,
Redhill, Surrey.

CHAPTER ONE

"How I wish I hadn't come," thought Jacky furiously. "If only I'd known that Mrs Marshall had broken her wrist and *she* was going to take us! What right has she to take the Pony Club? She can't even ride."

Jacky pulled her hard hat farther down over her eyes and scowled through the driving March rain to where the fat shape of Mrs Grunter, helped by two children, was setting up jumps made out of tin cans, wooden boxes and poles.

Jacky Munro was eleven. She was small for her age but wiry and full of energy. More than anything in the world she loved ponies and riding and some day she was positive that she would be chosen to jump for Britain—some day. But just now she didn't even have a pony of her own. It was Saturday afternoon and with twelve other members of the Tarentshire branch of the Pony Club Jacky sat waiting to jump while Mrs Grunter fussed over the height of the tin cans.

"It's just a complete waste," Jacky muttered to herself. "And probably Miss Henderson won't be able to let me have Maverick again now that the riding school will be busier at the weekends. Oh why did Mrs Marshall have to come off Sultan?"

Schooling under Mrs Grunter had been bad enough, but trying to make Maverick jump would be worse. Mrs Grunter had been very rude about Maverick, the pony Jacky had hired from the riding school. "Wake him up," she had shouted. "Everyone look at Jacky Munro. Here is an example of a completely unbalanced horse and a

5

lazy rider. Never let me see any of you allowing your ponies to crawl like that."

Remembering, Jacky snorted indignantly. "If Mrs Grunter had to work as hard as the ponies at the riding school she wouldn't be so fat and I bet she'd crawl round if she got the chance. Maverick doesn't need waking up, what he needs is a good feed of oats and a warm stable instead of a cold field."

Jacky looked round at the other children's ponies. Even the shaggy ones who must have wintered out looked plump and cheeky, and several who were clipped and stabled looked like little racehorses.

Jacky sighed aloud with jealousy. Maybe she shouldn't have brought Maverick to the rally. After a winter of too much work and too little food his bones poked under his long winter coat, his shoes were worn thin and like nearly all the ponies at Miss Henderson's he was old—fifteen or sixteen. "But if I don't ride the school ponies what am I going to ride?" Jacky thought.

Suddenly she realized that the six jumps were ready and Mrs Grunter was calling her daughter's name to jump first.

"Mummy's little darling," Anne Flynn whispered to Jacky.

"Hope she comes off," Jacky agreed.

Celia Grunter was ten, and fat and bossy like her mother. She was a hopeless rider but always won things because her parents bought ponies that other children had trained, then, when Celia's heavy hands and bad riding had ruined them, sold them again.

Today Celia was riding a black pony with three white socks that Mr Grunter had bought in Ireland a month before. The pony cleared the jumps without any effort and Celia rode back grinning.

"Well ridden, Celia," shouted Mrs Grunter. "Clear round."

"Well jumped, Prince," said Anne Flynn.

"Well bought, Daddy," mocked William Davis, a blond boy who rode a New Forest pony.

Jacky gripped Maverick's reins between numb fingers. Watching Celia and Prince she hadn't really seen them, she had seen herself in the future riding Miss Henderson's Flicka. Someday Flicka would be the best pony in the world.

William poked Jacky with his crop. "You're next."

"Jacqueline Munro! I have more to do than stand here waiting for you. Come along. You'd better come next. I expect we'll have quite a bit of bother trying to get you to jump."

Jacky gathered up her reins and urged Maverick into life. The old pony moved forward at a slow walk. Jacky felt him tired and unwilling under her. If it had been Mrs Marshall she would have explained and not jumped but she could imagine the fuss Mrs Grunter would make if she said she wasn't jumping.

Maverick approached the first jump at a slow trot.

"Wake him up! Wake him up!" yelled Mrs Grunter. "He'll stop if you don't."

Maverick stopped. Jacky turned him round to try again.

"Ride him at it!" Mrs Grunter's face was scarlet under her tweed hat. "Show some life."

Again Maverick trotted slowly up to the jump and stopped.

"Oh, really, child! When will you realize that to ride you must be awake."

"I am awake," Jacky muttered, turning the reluctant Maverick round for a third attempt.

"Now ride him at it. Get him going on a bit."

Again Maverick refused.

Mrs Grunter came pounding across to them.

"I'm not going to jump. He's not fit . . ." Jacky began but Mrs Grunter's voice drowned hers.

"Jump off," Mrs Grunter commanded. "Celia's going to

7

take him round for you. Just to let you see that a real rider can get any horse going."

Jacky gazed in horror, then realized that Celia was standing waiting to mount. Jacky sat frozen to the saddle. She wanted to shout that Celia wasn't going to ride her pony; that it wasn't Maverick's fault that he wouldn't jump.

"Come along now," boomed Mrs Grunter and somehow, against her will, Jacky was standing on the ground while Celia climbed up on to Maverick.

"Wake him up," ordered her mother. "Let him know who's boss."

Celia pulled at Maverick's reins, banging his mouth with the bit until the pony threw up his head. Her booted feet kicked into his sides and her crop rattled against his ribs.

"That's the stuff," encouraged Mrs Grunter.

Jacky had been standing trying not to watch. Suddenly she could bear it no longer. She raced across to Maverick and grabbed his bridle.

"Get off my pony," she screamed and snatched the crop out of Celia's gloved hand. "Don't you dare hit him like that!" She felt Mrs Grunter grip her shoulder and realized that all the other children were staring at her in amazement but she didn't care. She had only one thought in her mind, to make Celia get off Maverick. She waved the crop in Celia's face. "Get off him or I'll hit you," she heard her own voice shouting.

Hurriedly Celia scrambled down.

"If you knew anything about ponies you wouldn't let her treat him like that," Jacky stormed at Mrs Grunter.

"What an exhibition! My dear child, control yourself. Mrs Marshall warned me about your impulsive nature but really . . ."

"I'm going home and I'm never coming to another rally if you're taking it," Jacky yelled.

Her legs felt rubbery and she could hardly climb back into the saddle. As she rode through the field gate she realized that she was crying. She ran her hand down Maverick's neck and patted his side. "It's all my fault. I should never have taken you. Poor Maverick."

Maverick, knowing he was going home, walked out briskly. Soon they were clear of Tarent and riding between trees and high hedges with country sounds reaching them through the rainy dusk.

As she rode, Jacky went over and over the afternoon's happenings in her mind. "Beastly woman, but I suppose I shall have to apologize the next time I see her," she decided and started to think about the riding school. How bad things had been that winter; not enough food for the ponies; horses going out for rides with shoes loose or missing; tack breaking and being tied together with bits of string and Miss Henderson always cross and worried with too much work to do.

Then Jacky thought of Flicka and smiled into the gathering dark. If it hadn't been for Flicka Jacky would have changed to another riding school. Flicka was a five-year-old black pony just under 13.2 hands high. Her mother had been a Fell mare and her sire a show pony. Miss Henderson had brought her as a yearling and now that she was old enough, maybe this summer, Jacky was going to show jump her. Miss Henderson had promised.

Thinking about Flicka, Jacky forgot all about her afternoon at the Pony Club, forgot about the state of the riding school and forgot that Flicka in spite of all Jacky's titbits was really as thin as all the other riding school ponies. Jacky saw her sleek and shining with a red rosette flapping from her bridle.

Maverick broke into a trot, swung round the last bend in the road and the riding school lay in front of them. Light was streaming from the window of the front room of Miss Henderson's bungalow.

"Strange," Jacky thought. "She never ever uses that room," and she shivered uncontrollably as a goose walked over her grave.

Parked in front of the bungalow was a low-slung, black car. As Jacky rode past it into the stable yard she wondered who it could belong to. It was a stranger's car, not one that belonged to any of the riding school's pupils.

The stables and yard were deserted. Normally at this time Miss Henderson was busy in the tack room or sweeping out the boxes. Usually a few children were still hanging about after their ride helping Miss Henderson or waiting for their parents. Tonight there was nothing but silence, and darkness creeping in from the fields.

Jacky took off Maverick's tack, gave him the apples and carrots which she had bought for him and led him to his field. The ponies were grouped round the gate hoping for hay. Jacky chased them back, opened the gate and led Maverick through. As she slipped the halter over his ears something at the far end of the field caught her eye. In the dusk a dim shape was struggling and fighting. As Jacky stared she heard a high-pitched twanging noise. The dark shape seemed to be caught in the far corner of the field. The corner where workmen, only that morning, had been winding barbed wire round the telegraph pole that stood there.

Instantly Jacky checked the group of ponies. First she looked for Flicka and her heart leapt with relief when she saw that she was safely there. Kirsty, Sceptre, Friday, Dinkie, Bunter and Maverick were all there but there was no Dimsie—Dimsie, the valuable brood mare who had been left with Miss Henderson while her owners spent the winter in Spain. When there was any chance of food Dimsie was always the first to push her way in but tonight she wasn't at the gate.

Jacky charged across the field, stumbling into mud and over tufts of weed and as she ran the twanging of wire grew louder.

CHAPTER TWO

"You've got to come at once! It's Dimsie. She's caught up in barbed wire," and Jacky gasped for breath. She stood in the doorway of Miss Henderson's front room, dazzled by the sudden glare of light. "You must come at once."

Miss Henderson and the smartly dressed young man that she had been talking to looked up in amazement.

"Dimsie? But I saw her only an hour ago," Miss Henderson said, "Are you sure, Jacky?"

"Positive. It's her hind legs. She's caught in a coil of wire the workmen must have left behind this morning."

"Oh no," groaned Miss Henderson. "I'll need to go," she said, turning to the young man. "Could you come back next week?"

The young man scowled, picked up his hat and stuck it on the back of his head.

"Got to get this fixed up," he said crossly. "Either yes or no. I've got to get things straight, either one way or the other."

"Please," pleaded Jacky. "Do hurry. Her legs are terribly torn. I couldn't do anything for her by myself."

Miss Henderson stood up and pushed her hand through her short, greying hair.

"I'll let you have a definite decision at the beginning of the week," she said wearily.

"Monday?" demanded the young man.

"Monday."

As Miss Henderson collected wire cutters from her tool drawer Jacky heard the young man's car swing away from

11

the bungalow. She longed to ask Miss Henderson all the questions that were running through her mind. Who was the strange young man? What was it that he had to know by Monday? But Miss Henderson said nothing.

Together they hurried out into the deserted yard.

"Just my bloomin' luck," Miss Henderson muttered as they ran across the field towards the dark shape of Dimsie.

When they reached the pony she nickered softly, recognizing Miss Henderson.

"Whoa, little girl," Miss Henderson murmured, slipping a halter over Dimsie's head. "Oh what a mess!" she gasped as she swung the torch beam on to Dimsie's hind legs. "Oh pony, pony! What did you have to go and do this for?"

Dimsie had stopped struggling and was standing still with her head low. Jacky could hardly breathe for the lump choking in her throat. She hated the workmen for leaving the roll of wire in the field.

"Hold her for me, Jacky," Miss Henderson said, handing Jacky the halter rope. "And I'll see if I can get her free."

Skilfully, talking all the time to the pony, Miss Henderson clipped at the tangled wire. The pony didn't move. Even when she was completely freed she just stood there, her head drooping forlornly, the blood running down her legs.

"Need to get the vet," said Miss Henderson. "You run on and phone. Tarent 223. Tell him it's urgent. He must come at once."

Jacky ran back to the house while Miss Henderson led Dimsie slowly across the field.

"He's coming straight away," Jacky said as she came back from phoning to find Miss Henderson bandaging large pads of cotton wool round Dimsie's legs while the pony stood shivering in a corner of a loosebox.

"Thank goodness he was in. I suppose I'll need to let Major Campbell know. I promised Dimsie's owner that if anything happened to her pony while she was away I'd phone the major."

Jacky remembered the booming, scarlet-faced major who always stood at the ringside at shows criticizing other people's riding.

"Stay with her till I phone. We can't do any more for her until the vet comes."

Jacky stayed, stroking Dimsie's neck and talking softly to her.

"He's coming," Miss Henderson announced when she came back a few minutes later. "Pretty bad show, what? Wire left in a pony's field. Be over right away," she said, being the major.

But it was the vet who arrived first. He was a little man, quick and bouncy as a sparrow.

"Poor old lady," he said when he'd looked at Dimsie's legs. "However did you get yourself into this mess? Stupid woman! Need to stitch her up," he added to Miss Henderson. "She's torn a ligament. Be a month or two before she's back to normal, maybe longer."

Jacky held Dimsie's halter rope while Miss Henderson helped the vet. He worked with sure, swift fingers, skilfully and gently, while the bare electric light bulb cast giant shadows on the walls.

"It's like a dream," Jacky thought. "Like a nightmare."

At last the vet stood up. "There," he said, "that's the best I can do for her. Just see that . . ."

But his voice was drowned by the sudden scrunch of a horsebox coming into the yard. There was a screech of brakes and a man jumped down from the cab slamming the door behind himself.

"What's this? What's this?" demanded the giant voice of the major. He came striding into the dimly lit box, broad-shouldered and tall. "Can't think why there should have been wire left in the field in the first place. Got her stitched up, have you?" he demanded of the vet. "By Jove, she has made a mess of herself."

13

The major strode forward and laid a hand on Dimsie's flank.

"Good life, woman, the mare's like a skeleton. Not a pick of flesh on her!" and he lifted Dimsie's long mane to show her thin neck and ran his hand down her ridged backbone.

"They always lose a bit at this time of year," said Miss Henderson.

"Lose a bit," echoed the major. "If it wasn't for the coat on her you could see every bone in her body! Looks as if she hasn't had a decent feed since she came here."

"Rubbish," said Miss Henderson sharply. "They're fed every day."

"She's starved," raged the major. "Starved!"

The vet, packing up his instruments, said nothing. Jacky, picking nervously at the end of the halter rope, knew that what the major said was quite true.

"She's not staying here another minute. Told Margaret she should have left her with me in the first place," and the major took the halter rope from Jacky. "Good job I came in the horsebox. Get her out of this dump before she falls to pieces."

"You can't take her just now. Her legs . . ."

"Better get her away before her legs fester," grunted the major. "Be safe to move her?" he demanded of the vet.

The vet said it would, as long as it was only a short journey, but although he agreed with the major, Jacky thought that really he looked sorry for Miss Henderson.

With the vet's help the major loaded the unwilling Dimsie into the horsebox and drove away without another word to Miss Henderson.

"Don't worry," said the vet leaning out of the open window of his car before he drove away. "He's a peppery old boy, the major. He's never tried to make a living out of horses."

Miss Henderson stood for a minute watching the lights

14

of the vet's car vanish into the dark then she walked back into the tack room.

"That finishes it," she said. "I'm not going on. The man I was talking to tonight wants to buy my land for a market garden. He can have it. I'm getting out."

Jacky had always thought of Miss Henderson as a young person but suddenly she realized that really she must be almost as old as her mother.

"But the ponies? What will happen to the ponies?" Jacky cried.

"Sell them. There's a sale in a month's time at Buckley. They can all go there."

"But not Flicka? You couldn't sell her? You promised I was to ride her, to jump her."

"Flicka too," said Miss Henderson wearily. "The whole lot of them. I'm through." And although she turned away quickly, Jacky caught a glimpse of tears sparkling in her eyes.

CHAPTER THREE

Early next morning Jacky cycled out to the riding school. She always spent her Sundays helping Miss Henderson with the rides—in fact, nearly all Jacky's spare time was spent at the riding school. She just could not imagine what life would be like if Miss Henderson had really meant what she had said last night and was really going to close down.

Jacky hadn't mentioned it to her parents. She'd told them about Dimsie being caught up in the wire but nothing else. Talking about the riding school being closed would make it real and as Jacky pedalled into the yard she just could not believe that in a month's time it would all be changed.

Jacky left her bike in the hay shed and ran up to the tack room.

"Oh good, Jacky," Miss Henderson greeted her. "I'm going for the ponies. Here you are," and she gave Jacky two rope halters. "We may as well bring them all in. I'll need them all for the morning's ride."

It was a bright sunny morning and as Jacky walked beside Miss Henderson she almost began to wonder if last night had only been a bad dream. Miss Henderson seemed her usual self, the same ponies were waiting at the gate to be caught. Everything was the same; yet everything had changed.

When they took all the School animals in Flicka was left whinnying after them. There was no Dimsie this morning to keep her company. Last night hadn't been a dream.

"Give them some hay, Jacky," Miss Henderson said when she and Jacky had sorted the horses out into their various stalls and boxes, "I'll go and put the kettle on and we can have a cup of tea before we start getting them ready."

When Jacky went into the kitchen Miss Henderson was pouring out their tea.

Jacky perched on the edge of the table warming her hands round her mug of tea.

"Did you mean it?" she asked hesitantly. "Mean what you said last night about selling all the ponies and everything."

"I did," said Miss Henderson. "I've been thinking about it all winter. It was a gamble from the beginning. Trying to make money out of horses always is. And I reckon I haven't made it."

"But it's spring now," Jacky said. "They'll not need hay much longer. Grass doesn't cost anything."

"They need shoes all the time; tack wears out; there's vet's bills to be paid. It all takes money. No Jacky, I've made up my mind."

For a minute there was silence in the kitchen as Jacky realized that it really was true. Miss Henderson had meant it.

Jacky took a gulp of hot tea. "But you won't sell Flicka," she said. Her voice despite her efforts to control it was shaking. "You couldn't sell Flicka."

"I must," said Miss Henderson.

"Well, could I buy her?" Jacky asked desperately. "I get two pounds pocket money a week and I'd send it all to you, every week and with birthday money and things . . . It wouldn't take too long for me to pay for her."

Miss Henderson shook her head slowly, half-smiling.

"I'm sorry, but it would be too long. You can have her for three hundred pounds. She's worth more but I'd like you to have her. Give her to you if I could but I just can't afford to. Can't possibly ask less than three hundred."

"I'll ask Daddy tonight," Jacky said. But she knew there wasn't much hope of her father giving her money for a pony. "And if he won't buy her I'll make the money somehow. I swear I will."

"You've a month to make it in and then they all go to Buckley. Now enough of this, drink down that tea and let's go and get them saddled up."

While Miss Henderson was out with the ride Jacky brought Flicka in and brushed her down. Then she fed her the crusts of bread that she had brought from home.

"Don't worry Flicka," she told the pony. "I'll make three hundred pounds. You shan't go to Buckley."

Jacky cycled home early from the riding school. When she got in she washed and changed into a dress, then, taking her school bag, she went downstairs and sat down at the kitchen table.

When her father came through she was working hard at her homework.

After tea Jacky went on with her homework.

"I've finished all my lessons," she announced at suppertime "All my arithmetic. The lot."

"If you did it on a Friday when you get in from school you wouldn't need to do it last thing on a Sunday," stated her father.

"What's the use," thought Jacky hopelessly. "I may as well just ask him and he'll say no, and that'll be that."

"Miss Henderson's selling the riding school and all the ponies," Jacky announced.

"That's sudden," said Mr Munro. "Bit of a blow. You'll need to find somewhere else to ride."

"All the ponies?" asked her mother. "What about Flicka?"

Mrs Munro had listened for hours to stories about Flicka and knew that her daughter's life revolved round the black pony. "You were going to start jumping her this year, weren't you?"

"Yes," said Jacky, swallowing hard to keep back her tears. "But Miss Henderson says she'll let me have her for three hundred pounds. Please Daddy, please will you lend

18

me three hundred pounds and I'll pay you back with my pocket money. Please?"

"No," said Mr Munro firmly. "I am not buying you a pony until you've passed your end of term exams. Then we'll think about it but not before."

"But it'll be too late by then. It's ages until I sit my exams and Flicka's to be sold in a month."

"Now we've been into all this before, Jacky."

"If you bought Flicka now I promise I wouldn't ride her until after the exams."

"Now that's just sheer silliness. And you know it is."

"Yes," agreed Jacky bitterly. "I know. I know you won't help me. I know you won't save Flicka. I know you don't care," and she turned and ran upstairs to her bedroom.

"Ponies!" exclaimed Mr Munro.

"She's so fond of Flicka," said Mrs Munro. "Couldn't you let her have it?"

"No. She doesn't work at school as it is. What do you think she would do with a pony to dream about? No, definitely not."

Next morning, on her way to school, Jacky stopped at three newsagents and asked if they needed anyone to deliver papers, but they all had regular boys.

After school she went round to Miss Doughty's and asked if she would like her to take Bonzo for a walk.

"Of course dear. I'll get his lead. Any time you want, come and collect him. I know you love animals so I always feel quite safe about Bonzo when he's with you."

Jacky clipped on the asthmatic boxer's lead. Then, looking straight into Miss Doughty's faded eyes, she announced, "I'm charging forty pence for dog walking. It's for a good cause—to save a pony."

Before Miss Doughty could object, Jacky was dragging the reluctant Bonzo down the garden path.

An hour later when Jacky brought Bonzo back, Miss Doughty gave Jacky fifty pence but said that she didn't think Bonzo would be needing any more exercise that week.

"I think he needs nothing but exercise," Jacky muttered pocketing her fifty pence.

Jacky knocked on one or two more doors asking if they wanted their dogs exercised but nobody seemed at all interested. One woman asked Jacky if she was a bob-a-jobber, and when Jacky had to admit that she wasn't, the woman said she was a disgrace and did her mother know she was going round people's doors begging.

When Jacky got home she found a jam jar and put her fifty pence into it and her two pounds pocket money. Even to Jacky's optimistic gaze it looked pretty hopeless. "But it's a beginning," she told herself, and she tied a piece of fancy paper round the outside of the jam jar so that she wouldn't see how little money there was inside.

Jacky didn't count her money for another fortnight.

"There might be fifty pounds," she thought hopefully, looking into her jam jar before she tipped the contents out on to her bed to be counted.

On the two Friday evenings a friend of her mother's had employed her as a babysitter and paid her two pounds for each evening. The first evening had been no trouble at all. The baby slept all the time his parents were out and Jacky watched their television all evening. The second Friday had been disastrous. The baby had started crying just after his parents drove away and, despite all Jacky's efforts to silence him, he didn't stop crying until they came back at ten o'clock. By that time the baby's face had stopped being scarlet and was more or less purple. Jacky had had to remind them that they hadn't paid her. "I should have got danger money," Jacky had thought, "having to expose my eardrums to that din."

She had taken washing to the laundrette, scrubbed a kitchen floor, written two compositions for girls in her class at school, washed cars, pushed prams and done more shopping than she liked to think about.

20

"I must have made fifty pounds," Jacky thought as she sorted the coins into piles.

But there was only twenty pounds ninety-six pence. Jacky counted it three times to make sure and then, in disgust, tipped it all back into the jam jar.

And there were only another two weeks left, two weeks until Buckley Sale.

"I don't see how I'm going to make more money in the next fortnight," Jacky moaned to her mother. "I've done everything I can think of this fortnight and people get mad if I go back asking for jobs too often."

"It looks as if you'll have to accept the fact that Flicka is going to be sold," Mrs Munro said.

"Couldn't you persuade Daddy to buy her?"

"Perhaps if your school report is very good he might reconsider it."

"It won't be," said Jacky. "Worse than ever I think and it's too late now to do anything about it. The Easter exams were last week."

"Oh Jacky, you never told us. You didn't do any swotting for them."

"I was trying to make some money," Jacky said, turning away and going back to her bedroom.

Jacky broke up for the Easter holidays two days before Buckley Sale. Her school report was not very good.

"I was top in English," Jacky told her father, drawing his attention to the only bright patch in her report.

But after she had listened to his comments on all the "Jacky must work harder," and "Does not pay attention," sort of remarks, there didn't seem any point in even mentioning Flicka.

After another fortnight of odd jobs Jacky still hadn't managed to reach fifty pounds.

"Thirty-six pounds seventy-eight pence," Jacky thought in disgust, staring at her jam jar of money. "I might as well have spent all my time with Flicka. Don't know why I thought I could make three hundred pounds. I wouldn't

21

even know how to steal it. There's nothing I can do to stop them selling Flicka, nothing." And Jacky stared rebelliously out of her bedroom window.

"It's all wrong," she thought. "It's arranged all wrong. I'd be far the best person to look after Flicka but I can't have her because I don't have three hundred miserable pounds, but any rotten old runty person who has the money can buy her. Well that can't be right."

For so long Jacky had been waiting for the day when she could ride Flicka and now it wasn't ever going to happen.

"It's just not right," Jacky said aloud.

CHAPTER FOUR

"This will be your last day, won't it?" Mrs Munro asked as she stood at the kitchen table making sandwiches for Jacky to take with her to the riding school.

"Yes," agreed Jacky. "Tomorrow all the ponies will be sold."

"You'll need to find somewhere else to ride," said Mrs Munro, trying to cheer her daughter up. "Perhaps you'll find somewhere better than Miss Henderson's. You were always saying that her horses were too old and they didn't get enough to eat. There must be other riding schools in the district. We'll find somewhere else."

"But it won't be the same," sighed Jacky.

"Nothing is ever the same," said Mrs Munro. "You can't go through life expecting things not to change. Only make yourself miserable if you do."

"But I don't want things to stay the same," Jacky thought as she cycled slowly out to the riding school. "I didn't want to spend all my life riding Miss Henderson's old horses. This year I was going to ride Flicka. I was going to start and take her to Pony Club things and jump her at the gymkhana."

"Look where you're going on that bike," a motorist yelled at Jacky as he swerved to avoid her.

"Gosh, sorry," said Jacky, realizing that she had been riding along in the middle of the road her head full of the dream of jumping Flicka, of painted jumps in the ring, the crowd's applause as Flicka cantered out after a clear round and the silken rosette fluttering from Flicka's bridle.

"Fat lot of good being sorry," snorted the driver, "after you've caused an accident."

Keeping well in to the side of the road Jacky pedalled on. The basket of her bike was filled with apples and carrots for Flicka. She had kept two pounds of the money she'd made to buy food for Flicka, the rest she'd given to the old man who played the clarinet in Tarent. Her mother had said it was a silly thing to have done but Jacky didn't think so. The money was no use to her and it would be a nice surprise for the old man. Listening to his playing was the only good thing about shopping in Tarent.

When Jacky reached the riding school, Mavis Good and Pat Nelson were sweeping out the boxes.

"Thought you'd be coming," Pat said. "Have you brought plenty of Kleenex with you?"

"Miss Henderson said you might be going to buy Flicka?" asked Mavis.

"Well I'm not," said Jacky. "So don't talk about it," and she wheeled her bike down to the hay shed, thinking bitterly that she shouldn't have come. She would have been better staying at home than being here listening to people asking her why she wasn't buying Flicka. "I expect they've all got hundreds of pounds in their bank accounts or doting fathers who are just longing to buy ponies for them."

Jacky went out to the field to give some of the apples to Flicka. All the ponies were grazing, scattered in groups about the field.

"Flicka," Jacky called. "Flicka."

The pony threw up her head at the sound of Jacky's voice, stood for a second with pricked ears and then came trotting to Jacky, whickering a welcome. She nuzzled at Jacky, smelling the apples that the girl was holding behind her back.

"Here you are," said Jacky, holding out an apple and feeling Flicka's breath on her hand as the pony fumbled with thick, velvet lips to take the apple.

Jacky stayed talking to the pony for a long time and

24

then thought she would fetch a halter and take Flicka in.

"Hi, Jacky," Miss Henderson called from the tack room. "How about giving us a hand with some tack."

Jacky hesitated. "I was going to bring in Flicka," she said.

"If we all help," said Miss Henderson, "it won't take so long."

"Oh, okay," agreed Jacky, coming into the tack room where the table was loaded with bits of bridles, dry, cracked reins and four old saddles that Miss Henderson never used.

"It's all going to Buckley," said Miss Henderson. "If we give it a rub up it'll fetch a bit more."

Mavis, Pat and a red-haired boy called Mike Thornthwaite were already hard at work. Jacky selected a pair of reins, hung them from a hook and began to wash them.

"So you're not buying Flicka," Mike said.

"No, I'm not," snapped Jacky. "And shut up about it."

"Is that final?" asked Miss Henderson.

"Final," said Jacky between clenched teeth. "I've no money and that's that."

"But I thought you were making the money," asked Mike laughing. "Going round knocking on people's doors asking if you could take their dogs for a walk and then making them pay before you'd give them their dog back."

"Shut up," warned Jacky.

"Miss Doughty told Mum all about . . ."

Jacky's tack-cleaning cloth hit Mike full in the face. He stepped back, caught his foot on one of the buckets and a flood of dirty water swelled over the tack room floor.

"Oh really, Jacky!" exclaimed Miss Henderson. "As if we haven't enough to do."

"What is going on here?" a deep, shouting voice demanded suddenly.

They all looked up to the tack room door and there, to Jacky's disgust, stood Mrs Grunter. She was wearing a black and white check trouser suit which made her look more enormous than usual. Her black suede boots were in danger of being swamped by the spilt tack-cleaning water.

"Don't tell me, Jacqueline, that you're having another of your temper tantrums?"

Jacky scowled up speechlessly at Mrs Grunter. She had been meaning to apologize about the fuss at the rally but the sight of Mrs Grunter's scarlet, bossy face was quite enough to make her change her mind.

"Get that mess cleaned up, Jacky," Miss Henderson said, then, turning to Mrs Grunter, she asked what she could do to help her.

"I came over to enquire about the ponies. Of course I've heard the sad tidings that you're having to sell up but don't worry my dear, I'm sure you'll find something else far more suitable than slaving away here. We should be quite devastated if Celia ever gave up her riding but I'm sure no parents would like to see their daughter struggling on the way you've had to here."

"What did you want to know about the ponies?" Miss Henderson interrupted sharply.

"What are you doing with them?" asked Mrs Grunter.

"Fat, nosey pig," thought Jacky, splashing Mrs Grunter's tweed-covered, tree-trunk legs as she mopped up the spilt water.

"They are all going to Buckley Sale tomorrow," replied Miss Henderson.

"That's what I'd heard, and we were just wondering if you might consider selling one of them privately. Naturally I'm not interested in any of your old crocks but I had heard that you had rather a nice, young, black pony. Could I see it just now? You know what a grand little rider Celia is . . ."

Jacky froze in horror. Whatever happened, Mrs Grunter must not buy Flicka for Celia to ruin.

"I am not selling any of the ponies before the sale," stated Miss Henderson.

"But surely . . ."

"That is quite definite. Now if you'll excuse me Mrs Grunter, as you can see we've a lot to do and not much time left to do it in," and Miss Henderson turned her back on the open-mouthed Mrs Grunter.

"A most unpleasant female," Miss Henderson said when Mrs Grunter had gone. "I pity poor Celia."

"But you wouldn't sell Flicka to them?" demanded Jacky anxiously.

"What use would Flicka be to the Grunters?" Miss Henderson replied. "Now let's get on with this tack and no more nonsense."

Jacky took her sandwiches down to the ponies' field and shared them with Flicka. When they were finished, the black pony wandered away to graze and Jacky lay back in the grass staring up at the blue distance, trying not to think about tomorrow. But there was nothing else, only that tomorrow everything would be over. Framed between seeded grasses, Jacky could see Flicka grazing. Seen from that angle she looked like a miniature horse carved out of polished jet. "I could pick her up with one hand," Jacky thought. "Pick her up and take her home in my pocket."

"So this is where you are," exclaimed Miss Henderson looking down at Jacky. "I've one last ride to take this afternoon. Nobody's riding Kirsty. Do you want to take her?"

Jacky hesitated.

"Come on," said Miss Henderson. "Better than lying here brooding."

Unwillingly, Jacky got to her feet and caught the ponies with Miss Henderson. Back in the yard she helped to brush them down and put their tack on. "For the last time," she thought. "For the last time."

The four customers who were going out on the ride arrived and Miss Henderson led out their ponies and helped them to mount. There were two teenage girls, a silent man with a beard who had ridden with Miss Henderson since the riding school opened, and Fiona Marshall who was in the class above Jacky at school.

Jacky mounted Kirsty and sat waiting while Miss Henderson tightened Bunter's girth and swung herself into the saddle.

"Right," she called, and led the ride out of the yard and down the road.

Jacky closed her legs against Kirsty's sides and trotted on to ride beside Miss Henderson.

"We'll go round the roads and back over the moor," Miss Henderson said.

Jacky felt her mouth spread into a grin. It was her favourite ride. She clapped Kirsty's hard neck and glanced back at the other ponies. They were all looking better now that the spring grass was through. Even Maverick was walking out with a long striding step, his eyes bright and his neck arched.

Miss Henderson urged Bunter into a trot and the metalled road rang to the clip of ponies' hoofs.

"I've ridden along here so many times," Jacky thought, remembering frosty mornings when the ponies had slipped and skidded on the icy surface, hot days of flies and sweaty ponies, the day of the gale when a branch from an ash tree had crashed down on to the road in front of the ride causing instant chaos, the day Spectre had shied putting a car into the ditch. All the rides blended together in Jacky's memory. "And now this is the last time. No more."

At the gate on to the moor Miss Henderson dismounted and held it open until all the ride was through. She hesitated before remounting, looking at the riders.

"I think you can all look after yourselves," she said to them. "Once we get up on to the moor we'll have a gallop round. Only one thing, try to keep behind me or you won't know the way."

They climbed the rough track up the hill and came to the crest where the moorland lay stretched out before them. "Right," called back Miss Henderson as she urged

Bunter into a canter. The wind tore at Jacky's breath as they plunged forward. Sure-footed as goats, the ponies galloped over the rough ground. Normally before she jumped a wall Miss Henderson would stop and let the ride jump one at a time but today she didn't even glance behind. Digging her knees into her saddle Jacky felt Kirsty soar and land and gallop on. The wall with the drop on the far side that had always seemed so enormous before, was hardly there as they leapt over it. Downhill they galloped, over the ditch, swung round again and out over a broad flat sweep of land. And in those moments nothing existed for Jacky but the willing pony beneath her, the surge and power of the gallop and the freedom of the open land and sky. They had escaped from time. No yesterday. No tomorrow. Only now. The drumming freedom of the now.

At last Miss Henderson slowed Bunter down. The ponies stood in a group catching their breath while their riders looked at each other, grinning, silent with joy.

Slowly, Miss Henderson led the way back to the riding school.

"That was super," prattled Fiona. "That's the most super gallop I've ever had. Wasn't it super Jacky?"

"Yes, super," agreed Jacky. But it was too late. As she rode back to the riding school, Jacky could see the ponies' field, empty now except for one black pony standing at the gate. Time was back. Tomorrow was Buckley Sale. Tomorrow Flicka would be sold. After tomorrow she would never see Flicka again. And there was nothing Jacky could do to stop it happening.

CHAPTER FIVE

The clock downstairs chimed half-past seven. Jacky jumped out of bed and scrambled into jeans and a sweater. She couldn't bear the thought of actually seeing Flicka being sold but she had promised the pony last night that she would come up and say goodbye to her in the morning.

Clutching a bag of apples, Jacky cycled down the road to the riding school. It was nearly eight o'clock. The cattle float that was to take the ponies to Buckley was coming at eight. Jacky pedalled faster, suddenly afraid that she would be late, that Flicka would have gone before she got there.

She dashed past Miss Henderson's bungalow and ran into the yard. It was filled by the huge bulk of a scarlet-painted float. The ramp was down and as Jacky arrived Miss Henderson came out of the stables leading Kirsty.

"Where's Flicka?" Jacky shouted.

"In there," said Miss Henderson nodding towards one of the boxes. "I thought something had happened to you and you weren't coming."

Jacky shook her head and pinched her arm to stop herself crying. "I'm just late," she answered.

"Flicka," she murmured, going into the pony's box. "Flicka."

The black pony knew Jacky's voice and came across to her, whickering softly. Jacky threw her arms round her neck and buried her face in her long thick mane. She couldn't believe that this was the last time she would see Flicka; that they were really going to sell her pony. As she fed Flicka the apples and felt her lips, velvet gentle against her palm, tears ran down Jacky's cheeks.

"That's them all loaded now except Flicka," Miss Henderson said. "I'm sorry, but she'll have to come now. The float man is waiting." And Miss Henderson slipped the halter over Flicka's head.

Jacky wanted to scream "No! No! No!" but she just stood watching, saying nothing as Miss Henderson led Flicka out of the box.

"It breaks my heart too," she said. "Especially this one."

Flicka followed Miss Henderson up the ramp, her ears pricked, her eyes bright and excited. Jacky had a last glimpse of Flicka's fine-boned head, wide delicate nostrils and dark eyes, before they swung up the ramp closing in all the riding school ponies. Miss Henderson climbed into the cabin beside the driver and seconds later Jacky was alone. There was nothing else to do but to go home.

"There's a letter for you, Jacky," her mother shouted. "We couldn't think who it could be from. A typewritten envelope."

"Oh," said Jacky, not caring if there were a hundred letters for her. None of them could bring Flicka back.

She picked up the envelope, tore it open and read the letter.

"I've won five hundred pounds!" she screamed. "Mummy, Mummy look! I've won five hundred pounds for my premium bond. The one Uncle Jim gave me. I can buy Flicka! Oh Mummy, I can buy her, can't I? Daddy wouldn't really mind. I can keep her on the garage patch. To begin with anyway."

"Well, what luck," Mrs Munro said as she read the letter. "No, I don't think Daddy would mind too much as long as you don't go crashing down to the bottom of the class. But will Miss Henderson let you have her? This isn't money you know. You'll need to wait before you get the actual money."

"Oh she will. I'm sure she will. But I'll need to go now.

I don't know when the ponies are being sold. If I don't go at once I might be too late."

"There's a bus for Buckley in ten minutes," Mrs Munro told her daughter. "But do be careful."

Jacky flung her arms round her mother's neck. "I will," she promised. "And thank you, thank you for letting me buy her."

And the next minute Jacky was dashing down the garden path clutching her letter in her hand.

Never in all the world had any bus gone so slowly. Jacky sat upstairs and drummed her feet impatiently on the floor until the conductor told her to stop it. "He doesn't know that I've just won five hundred pounds and I'm going to save Flicka," she thought joyfully.

Jacky heard the market before she reached it; heard the noise of cows and sheep and pigs, and men shouting.

"Please," she asked the first farmer she met, "can you tell me where they are auctioning the ponies?"

"Right the other end of the market, love. Right over there," he said, pointing with his stick.

Jacky pushed her way between pens of bleating sheep and groups of sharp-eyed farmers and ran to the ring where the ponies and horses were being sold. A bay hunter was being led in by a horsey-looking man in a check tweed suit.

Jacky stood catching her breath as the bay was trotted round the ring. The auctioneer's voice called out the bids, rising to the incredible price of one thousand two hundred and forty pounds before he crashed down his hammer and the hunter was sold.

Panic flooded over Jacky as she stood unable to move, not knowing what to do next. She didn't even know how to bid for a pony; hadn't even got any real money, only her winning letter, and the auctioneer wouldn't count that as money. She had to find Miss Henderson, yet, if she left the ringside, Flicka might be brought in and sold while Jacky was searching for her.

A grey pony that came into the ring next was sold for eight hundred and eighty pounds. With a cold clutch of dread in the pit of her stomach, Jacky realized that three hundred pounds for Flicka really was a give-away price. If Flicka was auctioned she might easily bring in more than five hundred pounds and then even Jacky's premium bond win wouldn't be enough to save her.

Desperately, Jacky looked round for Miss Henderson. She knew she must be somewhere; knew she had to find her but was too scared to leave the ringside.

"A fine young mare," shouted the auctioneer and, to Jacky's horror, Flicka was being led into the ring by a dirty-looking man in a torn shirt and jeans.

"Come on now, ladies and gentlemen, what am I bid for this one? Just the pony for your kiddy—sweet-natured, five years old, got a jump like a stag."

In the ring, Flicka pranced at the end of her halter, tossing her head wildly, screaming to the other ponies, her eyes rolling with fear and excitement and her sides matted with sweat.

"Two hundred." shouted the auctioneer. "Starting at two hundred. Who'll give me two twenty? Two twenty I'm bid."

"I must do something, do something now," Jacky thought frantically. "Now or it'll be too late."

She pushed her way round the ringside until she was close to the auctioneer.

"Two forty. Any advance on two forty?"

"Yes," shouted Jacky. "Yes, I'm bidding. I've got the money."

But no one was listening to her. The bidding for Flicka rose in seconds to three hundred and forty pounds.

"Three hundred and sixty," Jacky shouted. "Listen to me! I'm bidding!" But no one paid any attention to her.

"Three eighty from the lady in the fur coat," said the auctioneer and, to Jacky's disgust and horror, she recognized the fur-coated, felt-hatted woman as Mrs Grunter.

B

"You sir, do I hear four hundred from you?"

With a curt nod of his head, the man to whom the auctioneer had spoken sent the bidding up to four hundred.

"No!" screamed Jacky silently. "No!" For she knew the man as well. He was a figure from her darkest nightmares – the knacker's man who had haunted Miss Henderson's riding school offering to buy her horses. Sometimes his box, parked in her yard, had already held one or two ponies on their way to the slaughterhouse.

"I'm bidding," Jacky yelled. "Four twenty. I've got the money—I can pay."

"Cut along with you," one of the auctioneer's men told Jacky sharply. "Go and get your Dad if you really want to buy that pony."

Mrs Grunter sank her face into her double chins. The meat man pecked, his eyes fixed on Flicka, and the bidding reached four hundred and forty pounds. Soon the price would be over five hundred pounds and even if Jacky could make the auctioneer listen she wouldn't have enough to buy Flicka. Never before had Flicka seemed so beautiful to Jacky as she did now, shying and dancing in the ring.

"Please listen. I am bidding," Jacky tried to shout, but despair had tightened her throat and the only sound that she could make was a strangled choking. Beside Mrs Grunter, Celia's smug face simpered and smirked as her mother and the meat man sent the bidding up to five hundred and twenty pounds.

"Now you're talking sense," joked the auctioneer.

"Please," prayed Jacky. "Do something to stop them. She can't be slaughtered and I couldn't bear to watch Celia ruining her."

Suddenly Jacky saw Miss Henderson walk into the ring and stand at the auctioneer's side. In a flash, Jacky had climbed over the rail and was dashing into the ring.

"Miss Henderson," Jacky yelled, "don't sell her! I've won five hundred pounds. I can buy her now."

CHAPTER SIX

"What on earth are you doing here?" Miss Henderson gasped in astonishment.

"Please listen," Jacky said and explained what had happened.

"Of all the luck! Well I must say I'm glad you got here in time. I wasn't exactly enjoying seeing my favourite pony being sold to Mrs Grunter."

Quickly and without any fuss, Miss Henderson spoke to the auctioneer.

"Sorry ladies and gentlemen, the owner is withdrawing her pony. Not satisfied with the price," and Flicka was led out of the ring.

"Here," said the man who had been leading Flicka round, "what d'you want done with her now?"

"Jacky will take her," Miss Henderson said, and the man handed Jacky the halter.

"Oh, Flicka," Jacky whispered, clapping the pony's neck and scratching her behind the ears. "Oh, Flicka, you're really, truly mine."

"You had no right to withdraw that animal. I was still bidding for her." Like an outsize hippopotamus, Mrs Grunter bore down on them.

"I had every right," said Miss Henderson coldly.

"I'm quite prepared to pay up to seven hundred for her," insisted Mrs Grunter.

"I'm sorry but the pony is already sold."

"She's mine," squeaked Jacky.

"This is utterly outrageous. You'll hear more of this,

just you wait and see," and Mrs Grunter, with Celia trotting behind her, marched away.

"Silly old trout," laughed Miss Henderson. "She can't do a thing. I never put ponies up for sale without a reserve on them."

Miss Henderson took Jacky's premium bond letter and read it.

"You can send me the money when you get it. Address it to the riding school and the Post Office will forward it to my mother. I'm not very sure yet where I'm going to be. Three hundred pounds okay?"

"But I was going to pay the five hundred from my prize money and find the other twenty from somewhere. I'm sure Dad would lend it to me now."

"But we'd arranged three hundred before that. Be good to her, won't you? If you school her properly she'll take you right to the top. When I bought her she was going to be the pony that was to make my stables famous." Miss Henderson laughed, then suddenly turned and walked quickly away.

"Thank you, thank you, and I hope you get on all right." Jacky shouted after her, but already she was lost in the crowd. Jacky was left holding Flicka.

Feeling as if she would burst with pride, Jacky led Flicka across the market. She was sure that everyone was staring jealously at her pony and wishing she belonged to them. In her excitement, Flicka bounded from one side of Jacky to the other. She would bound forward to the full length of her halter rope or pull back refusing to move. Twice she barged into farmers nearly knocking them over.

"She's only young," Jacky apologized, hanging desperately on to Flicka's halter. "She's not used to all this noise."

She was even worse when they left the market. Every few minutes she neighed with a sound like thunder, throwing up her head and standing rooted to the spot to listen for any answering whinny. Traffic swerved to avoid her, blowing their horns which only made Flicka more confused than ever. She pranced at Jacky's side like a war horse with her tail held high, paying no attention whatever to Jacky. For all her life her whole world had been Miss Henderson's field and now, in one shattering morning, everything had changed.

At last they reached the quieter roads outside Buckley and then the country lanes that led, in a rather roundabout way, to Jacky's home, and Flicka settled a little, began to lose her eye-rolling madness and look about her more calmly.

Jacky's arms ached with hanging on to the halter rope. "You are a silly pony," she told Flicka lovingly. "Behave yourself and we'll get home much quicker. You'll have your own field now. At the side of our house. Daddy was going to put up a garage on it but he never did, so it can be a pony field now. Come on, there's nothing to be afraid of here." For no reason at all Flicka was standing rock solid in the middle of the lane. Jacky tugged at her halter. "There isn't a thing. You're quite safe."

Suddenly Flicka swung round to face the opposite direction, dragging Jacky with her, and there, far down the lane, came the swaying bulk of a horsebox.

Desperately, Jacky pushed at the frozen pony. "Get into the side. Get over, Flicka," she pleaded.

With frightening speed the horsebox bore down on them.

"Stop!" Jacky's scream was torn from her mouth as Flicka reared up, almost knocking her off her feet. Any second Jacky felt that the quivering pony would have pulled the rope out of her hands and be galloping away in a blind panic.

"Steady, steady the pony," she cried, trying to keep her voice calm.

Suddenly the horsebox was on top of them. Jacky heard herself scream, caught a vivid glimpse of the silver crescents of Flicka's shoes as she reared again, striking at the air as the varnish and chrome of the horsebox crashed past. Then, losing her balance, Flicka fell, bringing Jacky down with her.

For a moment both Jacky and her pony struggled on the grass at the roadside. Then Flicka surged upright and stood shuddering, bespattered with mud.

"The beast, the utter beast," Jacky was shouting as she too scrambled to her feet. "She could have killed us both. I hate that Mrs Grunter!"

For as the horsebox had roared past, Jacky had caught a glimpse of Mrs Grunter's fat face staring blandly out of the cab window.

CHAPTER SEVEN

Quickly Jacky made sure that Flicka hadn't hurt herself, but apart from the fright she seemed unharmed.

"Now perhaps you'll be a bit more sensible and get into the side when I tell you," Jacky lectured Flicka as she examined the huge bruise on her own arm. "Mrs Grunter could have taken you in her box if she wasn't so mean. I bet if the police knew, she would go to prison for dangerous driving, but no one would believe me."

They started off again on the last lap of their journey. After her fall, Flicka was more subdued and they reached home without any more accidents.

"You've been an age," Mrs Munro said as she came running out of the house to meet them. "But you've got the pony. Lovely! But what's happened to you? You're both thick with mud."

"We've been in a ditch," said Jacky. "She was dancing around and Mrs Grunter more or less ran us over."

"Thank goodness I wasn't there to see. Are you both all right? No bones broken?"

"No we're okay, but only just. Someone should report that woman."

"She is a lovely pony. Was Miss Henderson all right about your paying later?"

Jacky told her mother all that had happened.

"It certainly has been your day."

"You wouldn't have said that if you'd seen us both in the ditch."

"Probably not. Turn her out on the garage patch and come and get something to eat. You must be starving.

39

What about Flicka? Shouldn't she have oats, or something?"

"She'll be fine just now. There's more grass in our field than there was in the whole of the riding school."

Jacky led Flicka into the field and took off her halter. The minute she felt herself free, Flicka kicked up her heels and galloped to the top of the field. She paused to snatch a mouthful of grass, then galloped wildly back to the gate. In the nick of time Mrs Munro slammed it shut.

Standing watching her pony, Jacky was overwhelmed with the sudden responsibility. Flicka belonged to her now. There was no Miss Henderson comfortingly in the background to tell her what to do. "If Flicka doesn't turn out well it will be all my own fault," she thought.

"Wouldn't she settle better if we leave her alone?" asked Mrs Munro.

Jacky nodded, still gazing at Flicka careering madly round the field. "Oh, I do wish you were horsey parents," she sighed.

"Well, we're certainly not that," laughed her mother. "Come on in and have some food. She can't possibly get out. It's too well fenced and she could never jump the gate."

And, with a last long look at Flicka, Jacky followed her mother into the house.

When her father came home from the office Flicka was still racing round the patch. Sometimes she took two mouthfuls of grass instead of one but no one could have pretended that she was settling down.

Even at ten o'clock when Jacky slipped out to say goodnight to her, Flicka was still standing at the highest part of the field with her head high and her ears pricked. She whinnied and came tearing down the field to Jacky. Then, realizing that it was only another human and not a pony as she had hoped, she swung away, back to her corner and stood listening.

"She's lonely," Jacky thought. "All alone in the night.

40

first Flicka walked raggedly, starting and stopping
 to the strange weight on her back. But soon sh
 ed it and, remembering the schooling Miss Hender
 d given her last year, she walked obediently roun
 d.

at's a clever pony," Jacky praised her as the
 d by the field gate.

ll we go for a ride?" she asked Flicka. "Just a littl
 e could go down the bridle path. It's very quiet."

 out on the road, Flicka walked along with quic
 steps, her ears pricked, her head held high. Jack
 to herself with sheer happiness. Ever since she ha
 riding she had dreamed of this moment when sh
 e riding her own pony for the first time.

reached the bridle path and turned down into i
 ang in the high hedges and bluebells burned lik
 n the spring green of the grass.

love to gallop," Jacky thought, looking longingl
 track that stretched in front of her. "If only I ha
 !" She had often galloped the school ponies wit
 halter on them but she knew it would be stupid t
 ith a young pony.

st as if Flicka knew what her rider was thinkin
 e into a trot.

'd love a gallop too, wouldn't you?" Jack
 pulling on the halter rope to steady her.

nly Jacky heard the sound of hoofbeats comi
 e lane behind them. Flicka heard them too a
 oted to the spot. She neighed with a thundero
 sound and from somewhere behind them a po
 in reply. Flicka danced with excitement.

ve yourself," Jacky said crossly. "Every time
 ther pony you don't have to behave like a luna
 they going to think, seeing me sitting here lik
 potatoes while you do just what you like?" A
 it was Flicka she was riding, Jacky kicked

44

I'll need to find her company." Her father hadn't been terribly pleased at finding a pony installed in his garage plot. He had said it was too small and too disturbing for the neighbours for Flicka to stay there all the time. "Perhaps he's right. I'll need to find her a field with other ponies but I've no idea where I'll find one."

Jacky lay in bed for ages, straining her ears to hear the drumming hoofbeats of her pony, and when she did fall asleep at last, it was only to dream of riding Flicka over an unending show jumping course.

Suddenly Jacky sat bolt upright. This time the beat of hoofs hadn't been in her dreams. Flinging herself out of bed she darted across to the window. And there in the monlight she caught a glimpse of the galloping shape of her pony, a pony magicked by the light of the full moon. With flowing mane, streaming tail and sparks bursting from her metal-shod hoofs, Flicka was going back to the riding school.

Jacky looked at her watch. It was half-past two. She listened but no one else seemed to have woken up. She dragged some clothes on over her pyjamas and, wriggling into her anorak, crept downstairs. She picked up the halter from where it was hanging behind the back door, collected a slice of bread from the bread bin, pulled on her wellingtons and very quietly let herself out of the front door.

The light of the full moon turned all the world to silver. Jacky had never been out alone as late as this in her life before, but running along the lane thinking of Flicka she wasn't in the least afraid.

When she reached the riding school Jacky stood in the yard and shouted softly, "Flicka, Flicka." At first she heard nothing and then, from the direction of the field gate, came a shivering whinny followed by the sharp clip of pony hoofs and Flicka came slowly towards her.

"Flicka. Come on, lass."

Jacky spoke gently and stood very still, holding out the slice of bread. She was afraid that when Flicka saw her,

41

the pony would gallop again. But this time she only nickered and stretched out her neck to take the bread with velvety soft lips. She stood eating it while Jacky put on her halter.

"They've all gone," Jacky told Flicka. "It's no good coming back. You won't find them here any more."

Almost as if she understood, Flicka rested her head on Jacky's shoulder and blew warm sweet breath over her cheek.

When they reached the garage patch again Jacky opened the gate and turned Flicka loose. The pony walked slowly away from her and started to graze. Suddenly Jacky realized what Flicka had done.

"You jumped the gate!" she screamed. Her voice shattered the moonlight silence and made Flicka fling up her head in alarm. "You're only a 13.2 pony and you jumped the gate!"

Jacky stared at Flicka, hardly able to believe that her pony could have cleared the five bar gate, then she swung round to face the full moon and bowed three times.

"I swear by the full moon that Flicka is going to be the best show jumper in the world!" she whispered.

CHAPTER EIGH

"Really I don't see why I shoul "Miss Henderson rode her a few t she behaved perfectly. And she's go

Jacky had just finished grooming a dandy-brush but her own hairbru instead and now Flicka was standin the spring sunlight, her mane and as silk.

"If I ride you would you be g pony, and Flicka tossed her head u

"Right," said Jacky, laughing. " you'll behave yourself tonight if now."

Stupidly, Jacky had locked hers night and she had had to ring th parents. Even now she didn't like her father had said. He had even happened again Flicka would hav

"If only I had some tack," Ja doesn't really matter but I do ne had insisted that the two hundre winnings was to go straight into pretty sure he wouldn't let her us

Very gently she jumped up on very still, talking to her and patti wasn't in the least upset.

Jacky closed her legs against F

"There's a good pony," she s on then."

hard. Flicka plunged forward, then swung round to face the opposite direction.

As Celia, riding Prince, came into sight, Jacky was lying along Flicka's neck, her mouth full of mane. "Oh, it would have to be you!" Jacky thought furiously as she pushed herself upright again. "Out of the whole Pony Club it would have to be you," and she scowled as Celia rode up and stopped beside her.

"Having trouble?" Celia asked nastily.

"We weren't until you arrived," Jacky said, tugging at Flicka's rope and hoping that she would think of the garage patch as home now and be willing to go back to it. But Flicka, having at last found another pony, had not the least intention of leaving him. "Get on with you," Jacky muttered.

"Can't you manage her? We saw her making a fool of you yesterday when we passed in the box."

"If a policeman had seen you, your mother would be in jail for dangerous driving."

"Did we give you a fright? I expect it's your nervous nature. Mum's jolly glad now we didn't buy Flicka at the sale because she says in a week or two you'll be so afraid of her that you'll be glad to give her away."

Flicka, who despite all Jacky's efforts had been getting closer and closer to Prince, gave a high-pitched squeal and lashed out at Prince with a foreleg.

"Flicka!" Jacky shouted.

"You see, she's out of control already. I'm not staying here to have Prince kicked," and Celia gathered up her reins and urged Prince into a canter.

Flicka plunged forward and galloped at his side. Desperately, Jacky tugged at the rope.

"Get your pony away," shouted Celia. "I've told you I don't want Prince kicked."

"I can't stop her," Jacky snapped, furious at having to admit it to Celia.

"Get her away from Prince."

"I can't!"

"Then I'll do it for you."

Jacky caught a glimpse of Celia's whip as it flickered through the air.

"Don't," she screamed, then heard the whack as it caught Flicka across the quarters.

Flicka had been galloping before but now her speed was doubled. Her legs struck into the ground like pistons, her eyes started from her head in terror. Lying along her neck Jacky hardly knew what was happening.

Flicka burst from the bridle path like a bullet from a gun. She swerved to the right and stormed down the road. On the metalled surface her hoofs sounded like a hundred drums. Somehow Jacky managed to stay on top. She clung round her pony's neck with both arms and clasped her legs as tight as she could into Flicka's hairy sides. She caught vivid glimpses of people staring in amazement as they stormed past.

Jacky tried to speak to Flicka to calm her but their speed tore the words from her lips. She felt Flicka's coat grow sticky with sweat and her sides heave like bellows.

"She can't go on much longer," Jacky thought. "She must stop soon. She must!"

Suddenly two blackbirds fluttered up out of a hawthorn hedge. Flicka shied violently and Jacky was thrown over her head. For a second she was dragged along by the halter rope until it was torn from her grasp. Then she lay curled in a ball at the roadside, while Flicka galloped madly on, the halter rope dangling dangerously about her legs.

CHAPTER NINE

Jacky sat up seeing stars. At first she couldn't think why she should be sitting at the roadside. Then she remembered.

"Flicka," she gulped and scrambled to her feet. The countryside swam around her as if she had just been on the big dipper at the fair, but she gritted her teeth and started to run down the road. As she ran, pictures danced before her eyes; Flicka falling and breaking a leg; Flicka in an accident with a car; Flicka lost for ever.

There was no trace of her pony. Two lorries passed and Jacky stopped them to ask if they had seen a black pony running loose, but the drivers only shook their heads and looked at her in surprise. "As if I was asking if they'd seen a dragon," Jacky thought as she ran on.

At the crossroads she turned right and came to Oak Boking, a tiny village with only one shop that sold everything. In its window, Jacky saw her reflection and realized why the lorry drivers had stared at her. Although she couldn't feel it, she had cut her forehead and the blood had dried in a sticky mess, matting her hair.

The old lady who owned the shop knew nothing of Flicka.

"She didn't come this way, dear. I'd have heard if a pony had come galloping through Oak Boking."

Jacky retraced her steps to the crossroads. If Flicka had gone through Oak Boking there had been a chance that she might have found her way back to the riding school, but she must have taken the road to the left, which in another two miles joined the motorway. Jacky tried not to think about the motorway which stretched like a snaking desert through the green fields, and which was filled day and night with the roar of unending traffic; the motorway which meant death to any animal who blundered on to it, certain death to a runaway pony.

An open sports car came screaming up behind Jacky and stopped at her side. It was being driven by a young blond boy and, sitting next to him, was a girl who looked about the same age as Jacky. Her long hair was cut in a fringe and hung straight down to her shoulders but she had the same laughing brown eyes as the boy.

"Have you lost a pony?" yelled the boy, leaning over the door of the car.

"Oh yes! A black pony?"

"That's her."

"Have you found her?"

"She came galloping up to our field when I was schooling Firebird. We've got her in one of our boxes now," said the girl.

As soon as the girl mentioned Firebird, Jacky knew who they were. They were the Dawsons, Roderick and Erica. They had only moved in to Middlemarch, a large country house, a few weeks ago. Erica had joined the Pony Club but everyone said she was terribly stuck up, would only speak to Celia and wouldn't bring her pony to rallies because she had ridden at Windsor and Wembley and thought Pony Club things were beneath her. But she didn't look in the least like that just now.

"Is she all right? She hasn't fallen or anything?" cried Jacky, not caring if Erica *was* Celia's friend and a super horsewoman.

"Bit scared but that's all."

"Jump in," said Roderick. "Bit of a squash but you'll fit in the back."

Jacky clambered into the space at the back of the sports car.

"Tell us what happened," Erica said. "How did she get away from you?"

48

Jacky told them her story as they scorched along. "Of course, I shouldn't really have ridden her outside when I didn't have a bridle," Jacky finished, feeling that both the Dawsons must think her an utter idiot.

"How beastly of Celia," exclaimed Erica. "I can't stand her. She's always bragging about her ponies and how much her father paid for them. But fancy her doing a thing like that."

"Nasty little girl," said Roderick, laughing. "Shouldn't we introduce ourselves? I'm Roderick Dawson and this is Erica, my sister. We've only been living here a few weeks."

"I'm Jacky Munro."

"You're the girl who made Celia get off your pony," giggled Erica. "You were quite right too. Celia and I had a smashing fight over it and I've hardly seen her since. Really I was glad of an excuse to be rid of her but it's been a bit boring riding by myself all the time."

They turned up the beech-shaded drive to Middlemarch. It was an old house built of golden-coloured stone and had a thick thatched roof.

"I hope she'll still be here," Erica said as they all got out of the car. "She was terribly excited."

Roderick led the way round to the back of the house where there were four looseboxes built down one side of a little yard. Three were empty but from the fourth came the sound of crashing hoofs.

Jacky had just time to catch a glimpse of Flicka's head before she seemed to rear up in her box.

"Look out!" Roderick yelled. "She's coming over!" and the next instant Flicka surged over the half door of the box.

Jacky knew that if someone didn't catch Flicka at once she would be away again. Recklessly, she dashed forward and linked her arms round Flicka's neck. The pony half-reared, dragging Jacky off her feet, but she clung on, twisting her fingers in Flicka's mane.

"Hang on!" Roderick shouted, and he was beside her

pulling a halter over Flicka's head. "The little varmint. Someone will need to teach you some manners."

"Did you see her jump?" cried Erica. "Whee!"

"What a shock I got," said a woman who had just come up. "Really those little ponies are more trouble than any hunter."

"This is my mother," said Erica. "Mummy, this is Jacky Munro."

"How do you do, dear," said Mrs Dawson, smiling at Jacky. "I think the best thing we could do is to go inside for some lemonade to calm our nerves. Roddy, can you cope with that fireball?"

Roderick said he would put Flicka back in the box and this time he would shut the top door as well.

"Really I should go home," Jacky said, remembering her reflection in the shop window and feeling suddenly shy.

"Oh, do come in for a bit," said Erica. "Flicka will be quite okay."

"Poor Erica is aching to get to know some Pony Club people," said Mrs Dawson. "But so far the only child she's met has been Celia Grunter. And honestly!"

Over lemonade and chocolate cake Jacky soon stopped feeling shy and began to tell Erica about their branch of the Pony Club—which ponies were best at bending, which were best at jumping, and all about their instructor Mrs Marshall. Then Mrs Dawson asked her about Flicka and Jacky found herself pouring out the whole story.

"But my dear child, no wonder you came off. I've been tactfully ignoring that rather nasty gash on your forehead for I know how Erica hates me to fuss. Do you think the pony is safe to ride?"

"Oh yes," Jacky assured her.

"If you ask me, she's just lonely," suggested Roderick.

Jacky nodded. "That's the trouble. She has always been used to the riding school ponies and suddenly she's all alone," and Jacky took a gulp of lemonade to cheer herself up. Really she didn't know what she was going to do. If

Flicka jumped out of the garage patch again tonight her father would be furious.

Over the rim of her lemonade glass Jacky saw Mrs Dawson raise her eyebrows questioningly at Erica, then saw Erica smile and nod her head.

"How would it be if Flicka stayed here?" Mrs Dawson asked, turning to Jacky. "She'd have company here and we've plenty of grazing. Perhaps Erica or Rod could give you a hand with her. It's always easier to start off a youngster if you have someone to help."

Jacky's mouth opened and shut but no sound came out.

"There's Minuet's saddle and I'm sure we could scrape a bridle together somehow," Rod said.

"Oh, thank you," gasped Jacky. "That would be super. Absolutely super. I'd love to keep Flicka here. If you're really sure it would be all right."

"Course it would," said Erica. "Come on and let's put her out into the field and see how she gets on with Firebird."

CHAPTER TEN

"You are lucky living here," Jacky said enviously, as she and Erica walked down to the looseboxes for Flicka.

"Yes, it's great. Much better than where we lived before. We'd only two boxes there, in the back garden sort of thing, and a field we rented from a farmer. But here we've got more or less everything—the boxes and a feed house, a tack room and two big fields for grazing and one smaller flat field for a paddock."

"Super!"

"But no use if you don't have someone to share it with. Thought I'd go bats if I didn't get to know someone soon."

"You should thank Celia. She was the cause of Flicka's runaway."

"Celia!" exclaimed Erica in disgust. "We were going to put up a notice at the gate saying, 'All Grunters will be prosecuted'."

"I'll do instead," giggled Jacky. "Once Mrs Grunter finds that you're riding with me she won't allow Celia to come near here."

"That's the real reason we offered to keep Flicka," teased Erica.

When they reached the boxes they could hear Flicka charging madly round inside and whinnying shrilly. Erica fetched a halter and they opened the top of the box door.

"Watch her now," warned Erica, as the black pony surged towards the door, thrusting her head and neck over it and pushing against it with all her strength. "Get back with you. Go on back."

Jacky opened the box door a fraction and squeezed in beside Flicka.

"Now, now, now," she said calmly. "What a fuss about nothing. Stupid pony."

Flicka rolled her eyes and stuck her head into the air when Jacky tried to put on the halter.

"Stand at her shoulder and put your hand over her muzzle," instructed Erica. "You'll never get it on standing in front of her."

Jacky did as she was told and managed to slip the halter round Flicka's head.

"We'll put her in with our animals. She's used to being in the same field as other horses isn't she?"

"Oh yes," Jacky gasped, as Flicka danced and plunged at the end of the halter rope. "That's what's wrong with her."

In the middle of the field, Erica's chestnut show pony Firebird and Midas, Roderick's chestnut hunter, stood alert, their heads high as they listened to Flicka's excited whinnyings.

"Here she comes," Erica told them. "A new friend for you."

She opened the gate and Flicka steamed through, dragging Jacky behind her.

"Get up with you," Jacky said sternly. "Wait a minute, can't you?"

She turned Flicka's head towards her and pulled the halter off over her ears. With a plunge and kick of her heels Flicka was trotting over the field to the other horses, her head tucked in and her tail carried high as an Arab's.

The two other horses stood like statues while Flicka trotted right up to them. They stood for a second, heads together, nostrils almost touching, breathing in the strangeness of each other.

"Wait for it," warned Erica.

There was a sudden high-pitched, pig squeal from Firebird as she lashed out at Flicka with a foreleg, and instantly the group erupted into a flurry of hoofs, snaking necks and tossing manes. Flicka high-stepped away from them, snatched a mouthful of grass, then cautiously approached Firebird and Midas again, her neck stretched out warily. This time Firebird's warning squeal was less violent.

"They'll be all right," said Erica. "D'you want to come and see the paddock? We haven't many jumps yet. Only a few tin cans and things."

When Erica and Jacky came back from the paddock all three animals had their heads down grazing.

"She's a super pony," Erica said, watching Flicka. "I showed Firebird once or twice last summer. She did quite well but then she tore a tendon and I've really been resting her since then. Are you going to show Flicka?"

"Oh, Flicka isn't going to be a show pony," said Jacky, shocked at the idea. "She's going to be a show jumper."

"Can she jump?"

"She jumped the gate out of the garage patch," said Jacky, and told Erica about Flicka's midnight escapade.

"Well, she won't jump out of this field, that's for sure," Erica said. "Even Midas couldn't get out of here."

Looking at the field gate Jacky wasn't so sure. It didn't look any higher than the gate to the garage patch. But she didn't say anything, thinking it would sound like boasting.

Roderick took Jacky home in his sports car.

"I'll cycle over first thing tomorrow," Jacky promised Erica as she waved goodbye.

"We can start schooling Flicka," Erica agreed. "See you then."

Mrs Munro was too concerned about Jacky's head to listen to her tale about the Dawson's.

"You fell off on the road?"

"Well, not really the road, more the grass at the side," Jacky explained, screwing up her face as she bathed her cut head with T.C.P. "But it's the best thing that could have happened. If I hadn't fallen off I wouldn't have met Erica. You should see their paddock and she's going to lend me a saddle and bridle and help me to school Flicka."

"Do make sure you get your head really clean," Mrs Munro answered. "I wonder if you should go down to the doctor and ask him to have a look at it."

"Oh Mummy! It's only a scratch."

When Mr Munro came home from work he was very pleased to hear that Flicka had found a new home.

"The garage patch was never intended for a horse," he stated. "And certainly not for a raving lunatic like that animal."

"You're just proving," said Jacky, "that you don't know a potential show jumper when you see one."

"You could be right there," agreed her father, laughing. "But at least we should all get a good night's sleep to-night."

The shrill insistent ringing of the telephone through the sleeping, silent house woke Jacky with a start. She sat upright in bed, thought, "Flicka," and was jumping out of bed as she heard her father's footsteps going downstairs to answer the phone. Jacky opened her bedroom door and listened.

"Tarent 356," said her father crossly.

"But is it serious? It's three o'clock in the morning you know. Then hold on until I wake her."

But Jacky was already halfway downstairs. "Is it Flicka?" she demanded urgently.

"Erica Dawson," said her father, handing Jacky the receiver. "Your pony's jumped out again or something. Dratted animal."

"Hello, hello," said Jacky.

"Jacky? It's Erica. Flicka jumped out."

"Gosh," said Jacky. "Has she got away? Bet she's gone back to the riding school."

"She got into the feed house," Erica said urgently. "Stuffed herself with oats and when Rod heard her and went down to find out what was happening she was drinking at the trough. She's got colic, Jacky."

Jacky felt a cold shiver run through her.

"But I don't know what to do," she said helplessly.

"We phoned for the vet," said Erica. "She's quite bad. Do you want to come over? Rod will come for you . . ."

"Of course I want to come," cried Jacky.

"Be ready in about ten minutes then," said Erica. "I'll go back and stay with Flicka."

"Can I do anything to help?" Mr Munro asked, after Jacky had explained what had happened.

"You can't," said Jacky. "They've phoned the vet."

"See you put on plenty of warm clothes," said her mother anxiously. "I don't like it a bit, you wandering about at night like this."

"She might be dying," murmured Jacky miserably as she went to get dressed.

Jacky heard the whine of Roderick's sports car and ran out to meet him.

"I'll come over in the morning before I go to work, see how you're getting on," her father called after Jacky.

"Thanks," Jacky called back as she scrambled in beside Roderick. "Is Flicka all right?" she demanded tensely.

"Well, we thought we'd better let you know," said Roderick, swinging the car round and scorching back down the road. "She'd gorged herself on the oats and I don't know how much water she'd drank before I caught her. She wasn't looking too good when I left her."

Jacky dug her finger nails hard into the palms of her hands.

"Is colic serious, I mean could she . . . could she . . ."

"Once the vet sees her she'll be okay," said Roderick. "We usually keep a bottle of colic drench handy but of course when we need it we couldn't find it. Got lost in the move."

"Will the vet be there by now?"

"He was out at a farm but his wife said she'd phone him straight away."

Roderick drove recklessly along the deserted roads, tore down the drive of Middlemarch and straight down to the looseboxes. A light was on in one of the boxes and Jacky could make out the silhouette of someone standing in the box.

"I think he's there," she exclaimed in relief as they dashed over to the box. But it was only Erica.

"How's she doing?" asked Roderick.

"She's been a bit quieter since you went," Erica said.

Flicka was standing in a corner of the box, her head drooping and her eyes half-closed. Her black coat was curded with sweat and her whole body had the tight, tucked-up appearance of an animal in pain. She paid no attention whatever to Jacky and Roderick, not even looking up when they came into the box.

Jacky went over and spoke to her but the pony only swung her head away from her as if she couldn't bear to have anyone near her.

"Best leave her alone," advised Roderick.

"I can't believe it," gasped Jacky. "It's so sudden."

"If you'd just eaten two or three pounds of sour apples and then had a drink of ice-cold water to wash them down, I don't suppose you'd be feeling too good. And ponies can't be sick. That's what makes colic so serious," said Roderick.

Suddenly Flicka came to life. She staggered round the box, then began to swing her head, biting and kicking at her belly. The whites of her eyes glistened as she rolled her eyes in pain.

"Don't let her get down," warned Erica, shouting at Flicka as the pony showed signs of sinking down on to the straw. "She mustn't lie down."

Helplessly, Jacky stood and watched until the spasm passed and Flicka was back, standing with hanging head, in the corner of the box.

"Can't we do anything," pleaded Jacky. She couldn't bear to stand and watch Flicka suffering like this.

"Not till the vet comes," said Roderick.

Jacky turned to stare out into the yard, hoping the others

wouldn't be able to see the tears in her eyes. She waited, straining to hear the sound of the vet's car, but there was only the unbroken silence of the country night.

Roderick brought a rug, threw it over Flicka and packed straw underneath it to try and keep her warm.

They all stood, watching the pony, waiting.

"Come. Come. Come," muttered Jacky. "Oh, please come," and then, as if her words had conjured it out of the darkness, she was sure she heard the sound of an engine. "Listen!" she cried. "I can hear a car."

"I can't," said Erica.

"Yes, it is," said Roderick, listening intently.

In seconds the vet was hurrying across the yard towards them.

"Sorry I've been so long. Difficult calving. But surely that's Miss Henderson's black pony." He was the same brisk sparrow that had stitched up Dimsie's leg on the disastrous night a month ago.

"She's mine now," explained Jacky, and quickly told the vet what had happened.

Without any fuss the vet brought a bottle of colic drench from his car. He mixed it in a long-necked container while Roderick put a halter on Flicka.

Roderick held up Flicka's head while the vet put the bottle in the side of her mouth and poured the drench down her throat little by little. Between them they managed to make the pony swallow most of the mixture.

"There," said the vet at last, "that should do the trick. That's got enough of it inside her to sort things out."

Roderick took Flicka's halter off and the pony went back to stand in the corner of the box. They all watched her anxiously for another half-hour but there didn't seem to be any change.

"How about a cup of tea?" asked the vet.

"But shouldn't we stay with her?" cried Jacky.

"You can pop down every now and again to see how she is," the vet assured her as they all went into the house.

"You look a bit colicky yourself standing out here shivering."

Jacky went back to the box every ten minutes, and by the time the vet had finished his tea and came back to inspect his patient, Flicka was looking brighter.

"She'll live," he said. "Keep an eye on her for the rest of the night and I'll look in in the morning just to make sure, And I would advise you to check your fencing. Can't have ponies getting out like that you know."

"She jumped," said Roderick. "Cleared the gate my hunter wouldn't dream of facing up to."

"Did she now," said the vet, giving Flicka a hard look. "Miss Henderson knew what she was talking about even if she couldn't make money. Always said this one would make the top in the show jumping game."

"Shall we take turns to stay with her?" Erica asked when the vet had gone.

"Oh no," insisted Jacky. "I'll stay with her."

"Are you sure? She's looking a lot better," Roderick said.

"I must stay," Jacky insisted. "I don't mind being alone."

"We'll see you in the morning then," agreed Roderick.

In the morning, when Mr Munro found his way down to the looseboxes at the back of Middlemarch, he discovered his daughter asleep in the straw and the pony who was supposed to have been dying a few hours earlier, standing at a hay net munching contentedly.

"So this is where you are?" he said, waking Jacky.

"Daddy!" she cried, jumping up. "Oh, look at Flicka. She's better." And Jacky flung her arms round her pony's neck.

Mr Munro listened while Jacky told him what had happened.

"And how much longer is this sort of thing going to go on for?" he asked when Jacky had finished.

"It won't happen again. Once she settles down it won't happen again."

"But when," asked Mr Munro darkly, "is the settling down going to begin?"

CHAPTER ELEVEN

"She's completely recovered," Jacky said, three days after Flicka's attack of colic.

"Yes," agreed Erica. "She's fine now."

They were leaning over the gate of the ponies' field, wondering whether it would be too soon to start schooling Flicka.

"It couldn't do her any harm to do a little work," said Jacky, who was longing to ride her pony again.

"Give her less energy for hopping over that gate."

Flicka had jumped out once more during the day, but luckily Mrs Dawson had heard the clatter of hoofs and run down to the yard and caught Flicka before she had time to do any damage.

"Now she knows Firebird and Midas she'll stop jumping out," said Jacky hopefully. "She never jumped out at the riding school."

" 'Spect you're right. Let's catch her and try on the saddle and bridle and see if they fit."

"Good idea."

They took Flicka up to the yard and Jacky brushed her over while Erica looked out the tack.

"You know, I can hardly believe that you're mine," Jacky told Flicka as she brushed out her pony's tangled mane. "That you're really mine."

Under the long sweeps of the brush Flicka's black coat was soon glossy and her mane and tail fell soft and silken.

"It's a nice saddle," Erica said, bringing it out into the yard. "A proper pony show jumping saddle. Couldn't suit you better. Minuet was Roderick's and Grandfather gave the saddle to him when he started jumping her. She was about Flicka's size so it should fit."

Jacky held her breath while Erica slid the saddle down on to Flicka's back. It fitted perfectly. Jacky fastened the string girths.

"Not pressing on her withers?" asked Erica, putting her hand under the pommel of the saddle. "Get up and I'll make sure that it's not down on her back."

Erica held Flicka while Jacky pulled down the stirrup leathers and carefully mounted.

"Fine," said Erica, squinting to look between the saddle and Flicka's backbone. "Even with your ten tons on top I can still see daylight. Now the bridle. It's a bit scrappy I'm afraid, but it's a nice, big snaffle."

Erica put the bridle on and adjusted the cheek pieces until the snaffle was lying snugly in the corners of Flicka's mouth.

"There!" she exclaimed. "That looks a bit more like it."

"I don't know how to say thank you," Jacky cried, feeling as if she was going to burst with happiness. "I mean it's all so super. Whatever would I have done if I hadn't met you?"

"Well, don't start being all humble," laughed Erica. "Come on, let's take her down to the paddock and you can ride her round for a bit. Rod would be flaming if he knew "

"Why?"

"Well, really we should be lunging her and all that but I don't think one little ride could do her any harm."

They took Flicka down to the paddock and Jacky rode her round at a walk.

"I must be dreaming," Jacky thought. "I must be." So much had happened so quickly. Less than a week ago she had been certain that Flicka would be sold at Buckley and that would be the end. "Perhaps things are never as bad as you think they're going to be," Jacky told herself. "Perhaps we make them bad ourselves by always imagining that the worst is bound to happen. But this time it hasn't. The best has happened. The absolute best."

After she'd gone round the paddock a few times Jacky thought she had better offer Erica a ride.

"Don't be daft," Erica said. "You can't go giving people shots on her as if she was a bike. She's your pony and you'll need to do the riding. You can't chop and change riders on a young horse that you're schooling."

They started lunging Flicka the next morning. Erica showed Jacky how to send Flicka round on the lunge in a wide circle while she moved slightly behind her in a smaller circle. By the end of her first lesson Flicka understood the sharp command, "Trot" and the slow, drawn-out command to "W-a-l-k."

By the end of the Easter holidays she was trotting and cantering on the lunge without any resistance and Jacky was riding her in circles at the walk and sitting trot.

"You can't do too much schooling at a slow steady trot," Roderick had told her. "The lightest control by the reins and push her on into the bit with your seat. Teach her to balance herself."

Before Jacky went back to school her father had a serious talk with her about her lessons and Jacky had promised to try to pay attention.

"But it's so dull. Sometimes when its arithmetic my eyes won't stay open. I'm trying to listen to what Miss Hope is saying but my eyes just shut and I think my ears shut too."

Mr Munro looked sharply at his daughter in case she was trying to be funny, but Jacky was quite serious.

"And I just can't do geography. No matter how hard I try I can't remember all those names. It's so boring."

"Learning about other countries, boring?"

"Well, it won't be when I'm jumping for Britain and I'm actually going to the places," Jacky consented.

"Oh Jacky," groaned Mr Munro in despair. "Now listen to me, and I mean this, if I have any complaints about you not working at school, that pony goes. Now do you understand? I mean it."

"Yes, I understand," said Jacky, knowing from the look on her father's face that he really did mean what he was saying. "I'll work."

Jacky had a hard think about it. "But I must school Flicka every day and I'll need to do my homework or Miss Hope will send him one of her little notes." Then, suddenly, Jacky knew what she would do. "I'll school Flicka in the morning before I go to school. Do my homework whenever I get in from school and ride again if I have time."

"You'll never get up in time for that," her mother laughed when Jacky explained what she was going to do. "I can never get you up out of your bed in time for school."

"This," said Jacky, "is quite, quite different. And once I get into the habit, getting up at six won't be any different to getting up at eight."

Jacky kept her word. Every weekday morning she cycled over to Middlemarch, caught Flicka and schooled her in the paddock. At first it was a strange feeling, making herself do something that she didn't want to do. To begin with she longed to turn over and go to sleep again when the alarm rang waking her in the early morning. "It's for Flicka," Jacky would tell herself. "How do you think you're ever going to be picked to jump for Britain if you can't even get yourself out of your bed."

But gradually Jacky began to enjoy riding in the still emptiness, the tracks of Flicka's hoofs in the dew making it easy to school in figure eights and circles. And Jacky knew that Flicka was improving. She walked out now with a regular, even stride, changed pace without losing her balance, extended her trot when Jacky asked her to and cantered without any stiffness on either rein.

"Very good," Roderick congratulated her one Saturday morning after he'd been watching her schooling in the

64

paddock. "She has come on. You must have been working hard."

" 'Spose so," Jacky agreed, grinning with pleasure. "But it's really Flicka."

"Does it all by herself?" Roderick laughed. "Sure some whizz horse you've got there."

"I know," said Jacky happily.

Two weeks before they broke up for the summer holidays there was a Pony Club rally close to Middlemarch.

"It's mounted," Jacky told Erica, "but not really doing anything. A Mr Forbes talking about turnout and tack."

"Just what you want for Flicka," Erica said. "Let you ride her with a lot of other ponies but nothing that will get her too excited. I'll take Firebird. Her leg is quite better now."

The next Friday evening they rode to the rally together. Jacky had spent ages cleaning her tack and grooming Flicka. Now that Flicka had her summer coat she gleamed like black silk when Jacky groomed her. After a few months grazing at Middlemarch her neck and shoulders had filled out and her quarters were round and hard. Jacky remembered how thin she had been during the winter at Miss Henderson's. "I'll never let you get like that," she murmured, rubbing her hand down Flicka's neck. "Never."

"Two weeks and we'll be free," Jacky said happily. "And the exams are over and I think I might have done a bit better than last time. Might."

They trotted their ponies down the lime-shaded lane to the field where a group of Pony Clubbers had already assembled.

"No Grunters either," said Erica. "They've gone to Greece for a fortnight."

At first Flicka was excited by the other ponies, whinnying furiously if Erica took Firebird away from her and glowering threateningly if any strange pony came too close to her, but she soon settled down.

"Last time I saw you at a rally you were riding an old skinful of bones from Miss Henderson's," William Davis said. "Is this one your own?"

"Yes," said Jacky nodding.

"Quite nice," said William. "I like black ponies best."

"Is that the one that jumped out?" asked Ann Morton. "She looks as if she'd be pretty fast."

"She is," said Jacky.

A Land Rover came down the lane and into the field. Mrs Marshall, Miss Hewitt and a man whom Jacky supposed must be Mr Forbes got out and came over to the children.

"Do you think he'll inspect our tack?" whispered Ann.

Mr Forbes inspected everything, condition and grooming of the ponies, the state of their tack and the turnout of the children themselves.

"Perhaps you can't turn a sow's ear into a silk purse," Mr Forbes said when he had finished his inspection, "but I'm going to show you how to turn a scarecrow into something a little bit smarter."

As he spoke, Marion Marshall rode into the field. Willow, her bay pony, was plastered with mud, her tack was filthy and she was wearing tie-dyed jeans, a fringed purple sweater and wellington boots, while her unplaited hair was blowing round her head.

After telling them the dangers of riding when you were dressed like Marion, Mr Forbes sent her away to smarten up while he demonstrated grooming and tack cleaning. When Marion came back she was very smartly turned out.

"They don't look the same," Erica said, as everyone cheered Marion riding round on her well-groomed pony. "You wouldn't even know they were the same pony and rider!"

Tessa Grey gave a vote of thanks and Mrs Marshall said she would be sending out the summer programme during the next week.

Jacky, who had been holding Flicka, mounted and was

glancing back to see if Erica was ready when Mrs Marshall called her over.

"Is that Miss Henderson's Flicka?" she asked.

"Yes."

"She is looking well. You've done a grand job with her."

Maddeningly, Jacky knew she was blushing furiously at Mrs Marshall's unexpected praise.

"Trot her round, Jacky, and let's see how she goes."

Jacky trotted and cantered Flicka round several times and then brought her back to Mrs Marshall.

"She's a nice mover too. Nice action. Have you done all the schooling yourself."

"Erica Dawson's helped, and her brother."

"She's a credit to you," smiled Mrs Marshall.

Jacky rode home from the rally in a daze of happiness.

"You should see yourself," said Erica laughing at her. "Grinning like the Cheshire cat."

"Over the moon," said Jacky. "And soon it will be the holidays and I can start jumping her."

CHAPTER TWELVE

"Did you get a programme from the Pony Club?" Erica asked Jacky on the first morning of their summer holidays.

"Yes," said Jacky. "Arrow trail at Craigie House next Wednesday, four working rallies, a visit to racing stables at Fenton and the Pony Club gymkhana on the 12th of August."

"Where's Craigie House?" asked Erica.

"Only about half an hour's hack," Jacky told her. "I should think I could take Flicka as long as I don't jump her."

"You certainly could not jump her. She hasn't started jumping yet and it would give her the absolutely wrong idea about the whole thing if you went galloping over walls in the middle of a herd of Pony Clubbers all being more or less run away with anyway!" said Erica sternly.

On the day of the arrow trail the driveway in front of Craigie House was jammed with ponies of all shapes and sizes. The smallest was a piebald Shetland grazing happily along the flowerbeds while the little boy perched on top pulled frantically at his reins trying to stop him.

Mrs Marshall came out of the house and began to shout instructions through a loud hailer. She explained that the arrow trail had been laid that morning by her husband and herself, and that there were arrows chalked on trees and gate posts, paper arrows pinned on to stakes in the ground, and arrows chalked on stone walls. She also said that there were plenty of false trails and it wouldn't be those who galloped fastest that would reach the treasure first. Anyone who hadn't struck gold by half-past three should ride back to Craigie House where cakes and fizz would be waiting for them. The greedier members cheered.

"Now if you'll all wait just another minute till I get Hobbit I'll lead you to the start of the treasure trail. After that it is up to yourselves."

Mrs Marshall mounted on her big bay hunter led them all down the drive, along the road and into a large field that sloped gently upwards to a little copse of oak trees. She waited until all the riders were through the gate, then, standing up in her stirrups, she shouted, "The trail starts over there amongst the trees. Good luck and be back in time for the grub."

Flicka was in the very front of the charge. She raced along loving every minute of it. When they reached the trees there were shouts of surprise, for instead of one arrow, three arrows pointed in different directions.

Jacky waited for Erica who was coming across the field at a collected canter.

By the time Erica reached the trees nearly all the other children had chosen a trail and trotted out of sight.

"You shouldn't have waited," Erica shouted. "I don't like letting her gallop over rough ground in case it makes her leg worse."

"Flicka was out of breath. Which way shall we go?"

"Not the arrow to the right," said Duncan Thornthwaite who had ridden up with Erica. "I remember that way from another year and it just leads to the quarry."

"Not the middle trail. Celia went that way."

"Then the one to the left," Erica said, starting to trot Firebird in that direction.

Behind Erica, Duncan and Jacky came the little boy on the piebald Shetland. He had been rather left behind when everyone left Craigie House because Midget, his Shetland, had still been unwilling to leave the flowerbeds.

They followed the arrows through the little wood, across two more fields and along the banks of a stream until suddenly the trail gave out.

"Why didn't we meet any of the others coming back?" asked Erica.

"I bet they crossed the ford," said Duncan. "Come on, we'll catch them up yet," and he pushed past Jacky and Erica, kicking his pony, Spider, into a gallop.

The ponies bucketed along, stumbling in the soft going at the stream's edge. Duncan swung Spider round and plunged across the shallow water of the ford. They all followed, splashing up cascades of white foam.

"Look," yelled Duncan, pointing to a group of riders that could just be seen in the distance. "They're making for the Crag on Haddon Moor. Come on. I know a short cut," and he was away like the wind.

"Stop! Please stop!" shrilled the little boy on the Shetland but nobody heard him.

Jacky knew that last year's treasure had only been a bar of chocolate and she rather thought that they were galloping their ponies too hard for any bar of chocolate. Erica seemed to have forgotten all about Firebird's leg and was urging her pony on.

Duncan pulled Spider to a halt.

"This gate's padlocked," he yelled. "We'll need to jump the wall." And he rode at the crumbling stone wall. As Spider cleared it and galloped off on the other side, Erica sailed over on Firebird, leaving Jacky and Flicka.

Flicka was standing with her head down, heaving for breath. Jacky dismounted, turned her to face the wind and loosened her girth. "It's your own fault," she told her pony guiltily. "You shouldn't have gone so fast."

Jacky waited until Flicka had recovered then began to ride slowly back to Craigie House. As she rode she wondered what had happened to the little boy on the Shetland. Really someone should have watched him but, seeing no sign of him, Jacky decided that the boy must have gone back by himself.

She had almost reached the stream when she saw the Shetland pony standing grazing, still wearing his saddle and bridle. Jacky rode quickly towards him, then something else caught her eye and she swung Flicka round to gallop to where the little boy was lying on the grass. His hard hat had come off and he lay with one leg strangely twisted beneath him.

Jacky leapt off Flicka and stood for a second staring down at him. She had no idea what to do. She knelt down and loosened his collar and tie and felt the steady beat of his heart but he was completely unconscious.

"Help! Help!" Jacky shouted, but no one answered.

Gathering up Flicka's reins, Jacky flung herself into the saddle and galloped across the field and through the ford. She knew she must get help at once, find someone who would know what to do.

Jacky had meant to ride back as quickly as she could to Craigie House, but after she had crossed the stream she saw a stone house standing by itself in the shelter of a clump of elms. Jacky turned and rode towards it.

"We've got to get help," she whispered to Flicka, urging her on. "Faster. Go faster."

She saw a boundary wall stretching between her and the house, hesitated only for a second, then rode Flicka at it. Without changing her stride Flicka soared over the wall like a bird, stretched to clear the ditch on the landing side and pounded on towards the house.

A wicker gate led into the back garden of the house. Again Jacky steadied Flicka then rode at it. Flicka jumped it freely and easily cantered on up the garden path.

In the drawing-room of his house Mr Spencer looked up in amazement, threw down the newspaper he was reading and flung open the french windows. "What's the meaning of . . ." he began.

"A little boy's fallen off his pony. He's unconscious and I think his leg's broken," Jacky shouted.

Without any fuss Mr Spencer phoned for an ambulance, found out from Jacky exactly where the accident had happened, phoned Craigie House and sent Jacky and his wife back to wait with the little boy.

"Best not to touch him when there's any danger of broken bones," Mrs Spencer said after she had looked at the child.

Jacky stood by, holding Flicka and feeling guilty. Really it was their fault he was lying there. They should have kept an eye on him, not gone so fast. But chases were like that, you always forgot about other people and were sorry afterwards.

Miss Hewitt, a Pony Club woman, and the little boy's mother came hurrying over the fields. The mother looked pale and kept saying that she had known all along that David was too young for this sort of thing.

At last the ambulance men arrived with Mr Spencer, lifted the little boy gently on to a stretcher and carried him back to the ambulance.

Jacky mounted Flicka again, said goodbye and rode slowly back to Erica's.

Erica was there before her and waiting eagerly to hear what had happened.

"They were all in a frightful flap when we got back to Craigie House. Wouldn't even let us eat our food properly. Chased us away."

Jacky gave Flicka a feed of pony nuts then told Erica about the accident.

"Did you really jump the boundary wall?" Erica asked in amazement. "The one with that huge ditch on the far side of it?"

"Well, Flicka did. I wasn't thinking about anything except getting help."

For a minute there was silence while Erica rubbed at her bridle.

"If Flicka jumped that today we could easily have her ready to jump at the gymkhana," Erica said at last.

"I was thinking the same thing," said Jacky grinning.

CHAPTER THIRTEEN

Jacky began Flicka's jumping career by trotting her over a pole lying on the ground. She trotted Flicka round in a big circle at a sitting trot then turned her up the centre of the circle, over the pole, circled round on the other rein and back up the circle over the pole again.

The first time Flicka goggled at the pole but trotted over it without any fuss. The second time she jumped three feet into the air and Jacky sailed over her head and sat on the ground seeing stars while Flicka galloped round the field. Jacky staggered to her feet, caught Flicka's dangling reins and remounted.

"Idiot," she told the excited pony. "It's only a pole on the ground, not Becher's Brook. Now calm down."

She let Flicka canter round, then brought her back to a trot. When she felt that Flicka had settled, she rode her towards the pole again. Instantly, Flicka plunged forward at a gallop, soared into the air over the pole and charged up the field. This time Jacky managed to stay on but not to stay in control. Flicka raced twice round the field before Jacky could stop her.

Jacky spent about half an hour trying to get Flicka to trot calmly over the pole but each time she took a mad leap into the air, unseating Jacky and then storming round the field. In the end Jacky was forced to go back to schooling her in circles.

"What's up?" Erica asked when Jacky rode into the yard. "You look a bit battered."

"We've been having a rodeo," Jacky said. "She's forgotten everything I've taught her." And Jacky explained what had happened.

"You can't expect her to know that she's meant to step over the pole," Erica laughed. "After all, she's used to jumping five bar gates and boundary walls."

"But the books all say that you start with a pole on the ground," moaned Jacky.

"I could bring Firebird down," Erica offered. "She's very good at cavelletti. It would give Flicka a lead."

"We could try tonight," Jacky agreed. "I've to go into Tarent with Mummy this afternoon."

Jacky wasn't too sure about how keen she was to have Erica watching her fall off Flicka, but when they took the two ponies down to the paddock in the evening Flicka seemed to have forgotten her morning madness. Walking and trotting behind Firebird she went over the poles without any fuss. By the end of the evening she was trotting calmly over four poles without a lead from Firebird.

"She's a dark horse," said Jacky as they turned their ponies out for the night.

"She was just letting you know that you can't have things all your own way," Erica told her.

By the end of her first week's jumping, Flicka was going over the cavelletti that Jacky and Erica had constructed, without any nonsense. Then Jacky built four low broad jumps and schooled Flicka over these. The pony loved jumping them.

"This is more like it," she seemed to be saying as she jumped gaily round the little course. "I don't know what you were messing about with those poles for."

Jacky increased the spread of the jumps and schooled Flicka over them every day.

"If Miss Hope made you work like this at school you'd all come out on strike," her mother told her.

"But it's not work," exclaimed Jacky. "I'd rather be riding Flicka than anything else in the world. And we go for rides. We don't school all the time."

Gradually the summer holidays slipped past and the Pony Club gymkhana grew closer.

Jacky built higher courses for Flicka to jump but went on schooling her over low spread jumps.

"Height doesn't seem to mean anything to her," Erica said. She had been schooling Firebird and had waited to watch Jacky take Flicka round a course of jumps they had built in the afternoon. "I've seen ponies that were good at jumping but never one that jumped like Flicka. It's no effort to her."

"I've told you dozens of times," said Jacky. "She's a show jumper."

It was easy to boast sitting astride Flicka in the Dawsons' paddock. Then Jacky felt sure and confident. There was nothing that Flicka couldn't jump. But lying in bed thinking about the gymkhana Jacky was terrified that she might do something to spoil her pony's chances. "I might take the wrong course," Jacky thought, "or fall off, or sicken her by jumping too much." Then she would tell herself not to be so silly, that it was only a potty little gymkhana, that it didn't really make any difference what happened; there would be other gymkhanas, other shows. But Jacky knew this wasn't true. It did matter. The Pony Club gymkhana was the beginning of Jacky's show jumping career. Flicka MUST do well.

"Go with you to buy summer frocks?" Jacky echoed incredulously, staring up at her mother. "But I don't need summer frocks. What I do need is a new pair of jodhpurs. I'm going to split that pair soon."

"Now Jacky, don't be tiresome. Of course you can't go on holiday without some respectable clothes. And last year's dresses will be far too small for you."

"On holiday?" cried Jacky.

"Now don't pretend that you don't know we go away next week."

"But I didn't," cried Jacky. "I didn't!"

"It was arranged at New Year. We're going with Uncle Bob and Aunt Moira, touring Scotland for a week."

"No, oh no," gasped Jacky. "I can't stop jumping Flicka. Mummy, I can't."

"You most certainly can," said her mother. "And I do not for one minute believe that you didn't know we were going. Not even you, Jacky, could have forgotten you were going on holiday. You must have heard us talking about it."

"I didn't," said Jacky dismally. "Honestly I didn't."

When Jacky told Erica, Erica said Jacky could come and stay with them.

"I wouldn't be allowed to. They think a holiday is good for you, though how sitting squashed in the back seat of a car being smoked over by Uncle Bob could be good for anyone, I don't know."

"It won't do Flicka any harm to have a rest," consoled Erica.

"But I'll only have five days until the gymkhana when we get back. Only five days!"

It rained most of the time they were in Scotland and Jacky sat in the back seat of the car between her mother and her Aunt Moira, thinking about Flicka and staring out at mist-covered mountains and mist-covered sea.

The minute they reached home Jacky dashed out of the car, changed her clothes and cycled full speed to Middlemarch. There was no sign of Erica so Jacky took a halter and went straight to Flicka.

"I'm back Flicka, I'm back," she shouted to the pony and, at the sound of Jack's voice, Flicka came trotting to the gate. "I've brought you some apples," Jacky told her as she rubbed her hand down her pony's neck and straightened Flicka's forelock.

As Jacky led Flicka out of the field she couldn't imagine why people went away for holidays when there was so much more to do at home.

The next five days flew past. Jacky's absence hadn't made any difference to Flicka's jumping. By the day before the Pony Club gymkhana Jacky built a course of eight jumps in the paddock and took Flicka over them. The pony jumped them all in her usual lively, willing style.

"She's a proper little speed merchant, isn't she?" said Roderick.

"I suppose she is fast," agreed Jacky. "Erica was saying that too. I suppose I don't notice it because I'm so used to her."

"She goes round the jumps like a tornado," laughed Roderick. "But it certainly doesn't stop her clearing them."

That evening Jacky and Erica cleaned their tack with more care than usual.

"Just in case Mr Forbes is judging the show ponies," Erica said, polishing her stirrup irons.

"I'll bet you Celia is there tomorrow. Probably be jumping in the same class as me," and Jacky swallowed hard, imagining how dreadful it would be if Flicka didn't jump or if she fell off in front of the Grunters.

CHAPTER FOURTEEN

It always seemed to rain on the day of the Tarentshire Pony Club gymkhana. Jacky had borrowed Roderick's riding mac because she hadn't one of her own. It was so big for her that it was keeping most of Flicka dry too as they waited in the collecting ring for their turn to jump in the novice class.

All my work's been worth it, Jacky thought, as she watched Avril Saunders' chestnut demolishing the jumps. Every minute had been worth it for the satisfaction of watching Flicka improve. And now it was the day when Flicka would have her first chance to prove herself in public.

"Still waiting?" Erica asked, riding up with a blue rosette she had won clinging soddenly to Firebird's bridle.

"It's an enormous class. The novice always is. There are still nine more before me but I think I'm nearly the last."

"D'you know who I saw? That little boy who fell off the Shetland and knocked himself out. He's got his leg in plaster but apart from that he's fine."

"Oh good," said Jacky, thinking it was an omen.

After five more of the novices had jumped, Jacky began to ride Flicka in. She trotted her in circles, working hard to make her pony alert and supple.

"You're not entering that mad animal of yours for jumping?" demanded Celia's grating voice.

Jacky ignored her. Since the day Celia had hit Flicka, Jacky hadn't spoken to her once.

"You'd have been better giving your entrance money to the R.S.P.C.A. because you haven't a chance. Prince and I are bound to win."

78

"Prince isn't a novice!" Jacky was stung into speech by the thought of how smoothly and professionally Prince had jumped at all the rallies that summer, but Celia was out of earshot.

"I don't care if she cheats," Jacky thought. "She's rotten enough for anything."

Jim Wilson on Chocolate was the last to jump before Jacky. When she saw him ride into the ring she rode Flicka over to the entrance and waited. Suddenly she felt cold with excitement. The moment she had been waiting for was here at last.

"Do your best," she whispered, leaning forward to pull Flicka's ears between her fingers and clap her pony's damp neck.

"I've got my fingers crossed for you," Erica said as Jacky wriggled out of the riding mac and gave it to her.

"The ground's like a quagmire," said Jim, riding out after three refusals at the brush.

Jacky shortened her reins, closed her legs against Flicka's sides and trotted into the ring. She gave her name and number to Miss Hewitt.

"Start when I blow my whistle," said Miss Hewitt.

"Right," and Jacky cantered Flicka in a circle.

"Now I should be thinking about all the things the books tell you to think about—the distance between the jumps and Flicka's stride and keeping my heels down," Jacky thought, but she wasn't thinking about any of these things. She could only think how glorious it was to be show jumping her own pony at last. "I wouldn't change places with anyone, not anyone in the whole world," she thought as Miss Hewitt blew her whistle.

Jacky turned Flicka towards the first three jumps down one side of the ring. She felt her pony full of life and longing to jump.

"On we go," she whispered. For a split second Flicka cantered on the spot and then she was away, rising easily over the white poles of the first jump, over the tin drums

79

that were the second jump and clearing with a great leap the hunt gate that was the third jump. Jacky swung her round the bottom of the ring, felt her pony prancing like a racehorse and then bounding forward to gallop up the ring clearing the next three jumps effortlessly.

"Only one more," Jacky murmured as she turned Flicka down the centre of the ring to ride her at the brush fence. "Only one more and we're clear."

The ground in front of the brush was a sea of mud, churned by the hoofs of refusing ponies. Flicka saw it, pricked her ears and took off at least three strides before the jump. Jacky was almost caught off balance. She bent swiftly forwards from her waist, squeezed her knees tighter against the saddle and let the reins slip through her fingers. Flicka arched high over the brush and stretched out on either side to land well clear of the hoof-pitted mud. Jacky laughed aloud with excitement.

"Jolly good!" exclaimed Erica, handing Rod's mac back to Jacky as she rode out of the ring. "She was super. She never looked like touching a thing. And the brush jump! Whee! It was like the Grand National."

Jacky slipped down from Flicka and gave her a handful of grass, imitating the professional show jumpers. Then, because grass didn't seem much of a reward when she had been so good, Jacky gave her a sugar lump as well. She loosened her girths and began to lead her round.

"Numbers 5, 8, 14, 17, come into the ring please," Miss Hewitt's voice rang out over the loud hailer.

"You're 14," said Erica.

"Is it a jump off?" asked Jacky, dropping Roderick's mac into the mud in her scramble to remount.

Jacky trotted Flicka into the ring where Celia and two boys she didn't know were already waiting. Mrs Marshall, holding a huge golf umbrella over herself, came towards them, making Flicka goggle and swing away in mock terror.

"Celia and Jacky were both clear," she said, handing her

umbrella to Miss Hewitt and taking a handful of rosettes out of her pocket. "Really we should have a jump off but seeing the ground is in such a mess we'll need to call you both first equal and split the book tokens. John Dunbar, third and Martin Barret, fourth."

Mrs Marshall pinned a red rosette on to Prince's bridle. "Very good," she said and passed down the line to Jacky.

"She's coming on very nicely. Keep her going and you'll both be a certainty for next year's Inter Branch team," said Mrs Marshall, hooking another red rosette on to Flicka's bridle.

Jacky made a gasping fish-out-of-water noise. She tried to think of something to say, but before she had gathered her wits together Mrs Marshall was pinning the green rosette on to the next pony's bridle.

"Just trot round the ring once," said Miss Hewitt. "The way things are going, the ponies will be wearing water-wings before today's finished."

"A certainty for the team! A certainty for the team!" Jacky sang the refrain under her breath as she trotted round the ring.

"Don't get in front of me!" warned Celia. "Really I should be in front. Anyone could see that your animal was out of control. I would have been sure to win if we'd jumped off."

"A certainty for the team," Jacky thought and beamed at Celia, hardly seeing her.

CHAPTER FIFTEEN

A fortnight after the Pony Club gymkhana the school holidays were over and Jacky was back sitting at her desk, wondering what Flicka would be doing at that particular moment and dreaming about show jumping, about doubles, trebles and jumps that were higher than she had ever jumped in her life before, while Miss Hope, in a cloud of chalk dust, talked about decimal division and adjectival clauses and the exports of Europe.

"Well, do you remember how to do analysis?" Jacky asked her father irritably after she had spent a whole evening struggling with an English grammar exercise which, even now that it was finished, she expected was all wrong. "When did you last parse a sentence?"

"Not yesterday," admitted her father.

"Then why do I have to do it?" demanded Jacky, stuffing her English grammar books back into her school bag and taking out her history text book. "And I'll tell you something else. Roderick says that Richard III didn't murder the princes in the Tower, yet there's a photograph of them standing waiting for him to come along and suffocate them."

"Painting," said her father. "They didn't have cameras then."

"But it's not true. Just a fairy tale. But I've to swot it all up. Probably this whole book is just a fairy tale. Probably everything they make us learn is just a lot of rubbish. I don't see . . ."

"Get on with it Jacky and stop talking nonsense," said Mr Munro sharply.

"It's not nonsense. Roderick says . . ."

"Jacky," warned her father.

Jacky propped her elbows on the table, put her fingers in her ears, stared down at the history book open in front of her and thought about Flicka.

Now that it was nearly winter the mornings were too dark for her to ride Flicka before she went to school, and by the time she had done her homework at night it was too dark then. Both Flicka and Firebird were still out all the time though Mrs Dawson had promised that when the weather was cold enough Jacky could have one of their boxes for Flicka.

"You'll only want to bring her in at night," Mrs Dawson had said. "She'll be better being out during the day."

Jacky had agreed knowing this was the sensible thing to do, but every time she saw Midas standing clipped and fit in his box Jacky imagined what Flicka would look like if she were in all the time. She pictured her pony standing in a thick bed of straw, her clipped coat supple as velvet over her hard muscles, her mane pulled to a silken fringe and her legs clipped out, fine-boned yet strong as steel.

Jacky sighed aloud. In reality Flicka and Firebird looked like teddy bears in their thick coats and heavy manes and tails. When Jacky did manage to ride it took her ages to take the mud out of Flicka's coat and even then she had to be careful not to groom her too much because the grease in her long coat kept the pony warm at night and dry in wet weather.

There was one mounted rally in the middle of November and, although Flicka behaved well and cleared all the jumps, Jacky knew that she wasn't going as well as she had been in the summer.

"She wasn't listening to me," Jacky said as she and Erica walked their ponies home from the rally. "She was charging round when we were meant to be cantering, and her backing was terrible. I thought Mrs Marshall was going to say something."

"For goodness sake stop moaning," snapped Erica. "Moan, moan, moan, that's all you do these days."

"Do not," snapped back Jacky.

"Oh yes you do. You can't expect a pony not to forget things. Once you start schooling her regularly again she'll be okay."

"But she was pulling like anything today. She never used to pull like that."

"It's only because she was fresh. You can't expect her to be perfect all the time."

Jacky didn't reply and they rode on in silence.

At the beginning of December there was an announcement in the Tarent Gazette saying that the Boxing Day meet of the Tarentshire and Westonlie Hunt would be at Threave House.

"Threave House!" Jacky exclaimed excitedly, nearly spilling her breakfast coffee as she spoke. "That's only about five miles away! It always used to be at Doune Castle. Always. The Boxing Day meet was always held there because that's why we could never go from Miss Henderson's."

"Doune Castle is a council housing estate now," said Mrs Munro.

"But Threave House. We could hack to Threave," and instantly Jacky's head was filled with the thought of hounds and hunters and of herself galloping and jumping Flicka over winter-bare fields and bleak stone walls.

"I'll need to phone Erica," Jacky cried, jumping up from the table and dashing into the hall.

"Come back and finish your breakfast," said her mother, but already Jacky was dialling the Dawsons' number.

"Engaged," she announced in disgust, coming back to the breakfast table.

She had just sat down when the phone rang.

"Finish your breakfast," said her mother, going to answer it.

Jacky gobbled toast and marmalade. "Boxing Day," she thought. "We'd have a week to get them fit."

"It's for you," said her mother.

"Jacky? Jacky listen," said Erica's excited voice. "I've just seen it in the paper, the Boxing Day meet is at Threave House. Close enough for us to hack to it."

"I know," screamed Jacky. "I was just trying to phone you to tell you."

"We'll go?" said Erica.

"We must," confirmed Jacky.

She cycled home with Erica after school. It was Friday so there was plenty of time for her homework over the weekend.

"Let's bring them in first," Erica suggested. "Give them a feed and then we can talk about the meet. I'll put their nuts in if you go and fetch the nags."

Jacky took two halters and went down to the field. The ponies were dark, shaggy shapes waiting at the field gate. As Jacky slipped into the field, Flicka bared her teeth, nipping Firebird's neck, and a sudden confusion of shaking manes and stamp of hoofs shattered the silence.

"Behave yourselves," Jacky told them sharply. "You'll both get fed in a minute. Get up Flicka. Leave her alone."

The two ponies clopped at Jacky's side as she led them back to their boxes, but to Jacky it wasn't two muddy, dense-coated ponies that walked beside her but two hunters, clipped and fit, prancing on their toes as the huntsman's horn sang through the air.

"Have you hunted before?" Jacky asked Erica when they were both sitting on the tack room table eating the pies they had bought on their way home from school.

"Rod took me with him once or twice," said Erica through a mouthful of pie. "He's not very keen on nurse-maiding, though."

"We wouldn't need him to look after us!" exclaimed Jacky.

"It's quite good having him," admitted Erica. "It's not

like a Pony Club thing you know. They take it very seriously and there's so many things you can do wrong. It's all very posh and superior but underneath everyone's a bit nervous and excited. All the horses know what's going to happen. You can feel the tightness of it all like a spring coiled up tight before it goes whee! into the air."

Jacky munched her pie. "We MUST go," she said.

"Where MUST you go?" asked Roderick, coming into the tack room.

"There's a meet at Threave House on Boxing Day," explained Erica.

"Ah!" said Roderick.

"Are you going?"

"Might be. If I'm sober."

"Can we come with you?"

"Come with me on those two hirsute hippopotamuses?" mocked Roderick. "Most certainly not."

"He'll take us," Erica said when Roderick had gone. "When he says no like that it means yes."

Once their Christmas holidays began, Jacky and Erica started to bring their ponies in at night.

"Lot more work," said Erica as she and Jacky mucked out after their ponies' first night in.

"But it gives us a chance to get them fit before Boxing Day," said Jacky, who didn't care how much work she had to do as long as she was with Flicka.

"Get them a bit less totally unfit," said Erica.

The paddock was too muddy for them to do much schooling, so most of the time they hacked their ponies round the roads at a steady trot.

"I do wish it would dry up," Jacky said as they rode past the paddock where the cans and poles were scattered in a sea of mud.

"Not much chance now until the spring."

"If only we had an indoor school. Then we could jump all the year round."

86

"Do you ever," asked Erica, "think of anything else except jumping?"

"No," said Jacky. "Not really. Even when I'm thinking about other things on top I'm still thinking about jumping Flicka underneath."

The day before Christmas Day Roderick offered to trace clip their ponies.

"I'm only doing it for my own good," he told them. "To try to stop the Master sending you both home whenever he claps eyes on you."

Firebird had been clipped out before and didn't make any fuss. She stood perfectly still while Roderick ran the whirring clippers under her belly, over her chest and up her neck. But when Jacky led Flicka out into the yard and Roderick switched on the clippers Flicka sprang away in alarm. At the rope's end she goggled and shied in horror. It took them nearly an hour before they could persuade the pony to stand still while Roderick patted her with one hand and held the clippers in the other. Then Jacky remembered that she had some carrots in her bicycle basket. She fed them to Flicka one by one while Roderick did his best to clip her. But even with the distraction of the carrots Flicka fretted and fussed.

"There! Take her away," Roderick exclaimed three hours later. "I never want to see her in my life again."

"Thank you very, very much," said Jacky. "She looks super."

"Well, maybe a little bit more like a hunter and slightly less like a cart horse," admitted Roderick, surveying his handiwork.

Christmas Day was filled with food and presents and being polite to relatives. Jacky's best presents were a pair of jodhpur boots from her mother and father and an enlarged, framed photograph of Flicka from Erica. Her worst was a pink frilly nightdress from Aunt Moira.

"As if I'd ever wear that," said Jacky scornfully.

"You will one day," promised Mrs Munro.

Jacky snorted.

That night Jacky set her alarm for six o'clock. "How awful if I slept in," she thought and went back down to the kitchen to get a tin plate to stand the alarm on. "Now I'm bound to hear it."

She lay in bed thinking about tomorrow. Her riding clothes carefully cleaned and pressed were hanging in the wardrobe instead of lying in a heap on the chair. Her hard hat was brushed until it almost looked respectable and she'd bought a pair of yellow string gloves although she'd never worn gloves before when she was riding.

Jacky pictured Flicka standing in her box not knowing that tomorrow she was going hunting.

"Tomorrow!" Jacky thought and visions of hounds and hunters made her shudder with anticipation.

CHAPTER SIXTEEN

"We'll trot on here," Roderick called back over his shoulder. "Take the tickle out of their feet," and he closed his legs against Midas's swelling sides and let his fit chestnut hunter stride on down the road.

Behind him, Jacky and Erica urged their ponies into a fast trot.

"Wait for us," shouted Erica, but her brother paid no attention.

"He's in a bad mood," Erica explained to Jacky. "Didn't get in from the party he was at until five o'clock and he couldn't tie his stock. Shouting and cursing and in the end Mummy had to tie it for him. She always has to do it in the end. Why he doesn't just ask her to do it to begin with and save himself going spare over it I do not know."

Jacky hardly heard her. She had no time for anything except Flicka. As if the pony knew something different was going to happen today she plunged forward, cantering on the road, tossing her head against the bit and shying suddenly at the least flicker of movement in the leafless hedgerows.

"Horsebox behind," called out Erica, and Roderick brought Midas into the side of the road but kept on trotting.

"Wave him on, Erica, the road's clear," Roderick shouted back.

Tucked between Firebird and Midas, Jacky heard the heavy throbbing engine of the horsebox draw level with Firebird and come crawling up behind Flicka. She sat down tight in the saddle, collecting Flicka between seat and reins as her pony tightened beneath her, cantering on the spot.

"Steady, steady," Jacky soothed Flicka. "It's only a horsebox. Steady the pony."

"Why doesn't it get on and pass us," she thought as the box continued to crawl along just behind Flicka. It was level with Flicka's quarters when Roderick turned round and shouted to the driver to get on past them. Jacky too glanced back and, in that second, Flicka's nerve broke. She stormed forward into Midas, there was a clash of stirrups and Flicka was away galloping up the road. Desperately, Jacky pulled at her reins. Sawing at Flicka's mouth she managed to bring her to a trot and turn her through an open gate into a ploughed field.

"You stupid idiot," she told Flicka crossly as, goggle-eyed, the pony stood staring at the horsebox driving on down the road.

"Well, that was a nice exhibition," said Roderick as he and Erica came clattering up to Flicka. "What did you want to let her get away with you like that for?"

"I didn't want to," stated Jacky. "Flicka just went."

"How many oats have you been giving that pony?" Roderick asked suspiciously as they trotted on.

"I wanted to make sure she'd be fit for hunting," Jacky answered, thinking guiltily of the big feeds that Flicka had consumed during the last day or two.

"She's fit all right," said Roderick in disgust, "and you look as if you've started your hunting already. Look at her legs."

Jacky looked down at Flicka's muddy hoofs.

"At least you got her stopped," consoled Erica.

Several other horseboxes and trailers passed them on their way to the meet but Jacky managed to keep either Midas or Firebird between Flicka and their looming terror.

The long drive to Threave House was lined with parked cars.

"Lot of followers," said Roderick. "Always get a lot out on Boxing Day."

Ahead of them a groom on a clipped bay horse led a grey and another bay and behind them a group of four women on greys talked in loud excited voices, comparing notes on their last day's hunting.

In the large space in front of Threave House the huntsman and two whippers-in waited like statues above the tan and white froth of hounds. Around them was all the bustle and churn of the meet: black coats and pink coats; red, weather-beaten farmer faces; women with smooth make-up looking like advertisements for Moss Bros; children in jockey caps and ratcatcher and foot followers in sheepskin coats and boots. At the edge of the crowd were the horses and ponies: grooms with stick-thin legs and walnut faces led clipped hunters up and down; children held tightly on to the reins of excited ponies; parties from riding schools waited uneasily; two women riding side saddle in immaculate black habits surveyed the scene through their veils. The morning was loud with noise, high-pitched extravagant greetings, the chink of glasses, the chirruping voices of the huntsman and whippers-in as they spoke to hounds, the sudden crack of a lash and their raised anger as they rated an offender and, flung like a banner high over the texture of noise, the sudden wild whinny of a horse.

Flicka pranced from the ground as if it were red hot, her neck was arched hard and high, her ears sharply pricked as she stared about her in amazement.

"Keep her well away from hounds," warned Roderick. "It is *the* sin to let your horse kick a hound."

Jacky nodded. She was feeling as excited as Flicka. She had never been to a meet before and it was all new and strange. She could feel the tense nervousness that Erica had talked about. They were all waiting; hounds, horses and people, waiting for the galloping and jumping to begin.

Roderick led the way to a fairly quiet spot at the side of Threave House.

"Don't let her dig up the ground like that," he told Jacky.

"I can't stop her," Jacky said. "Whenever we stand still for a second she starts pawing at the ground."

"Then keep her walking about. She'll be through to Australia in another minute," said Roderick crossly, looking at the hole Flicka had dug with her forefeet in the gravel.

The Hunt Secretary came up to them and they paid their cap. Then a girl that Roderick knew came over to talk to him.

"I'm going into the house with Sue," Roderick told them.

"Shall I hold Midas for you?" offered Erica.

"No, it's okay," said Sue. "Mummy's got my mare. She'll hang on to Rod's as well."

"Sue is the one he's keen on at the moment," Erica told Jacky. "I can't stand her."

"And here's someone *I* can't stand," said Jacky in disgust, as Celia Grunter in a black jacket and boots came riding across to them.

"Look at your pony," Celia screamed. "It's absolutely covered in mud."

"Yours," retorted Jacky, "looks like a Christmas tree, you've got so much tack on it."

"Oh I always ride him in a drop noseband and a martingale," Celia said scornfully.

"Then why are you wearing spurs?" asked Erica.

"When Daddy bought him for his little daughter all he needed was a snaffle," taunted Jacky. "But I suppose you *always* ride him with all that ironmongery shoved in his mouth."

"Darling," shrieked Mrs Grunter. "What are you doing? Do come here and meet Armanda Cuthbertson."

"Thank goodness," said Jacky. "Thought she was going to see all the holes that Flicka's made."

Erica looked at the scraped gravel. "Bit of a mess," she said, and she got off Firebird and did her best to spread the gravel back into the holes.

"I think they're going to start," Jacky announced as she watched the sudden flurry of action in front of Threave House.

Erica looked up from her hole-filling-in activities. "Gosh, yes," she said, scrambling up on to Firebird as the Master on a heavyweight bay hunter led hounds down the drive. Behind him riders crushed and jostled for places, fresh hunters bucked, ponies with heads down charged like express trains—suddenly the river of energy that had been dammed up in front of Threave had burst its banks. Nothing could stop it now.

"Where's Roderick got to?" demanded Erica as she fought to hold back Firebird.

"I can't hold Flicka back any longer," Jacky gasped. Her pony was plunging like a rocking horse in her eagerness to follow the hunt. "I'm going to come off if she puts in a buck like that again. Oh, come on Erica, we can't wait for Rod."

As she spoke, Jacky eased her fingers on Flicka's reins and, in a flash, the black pony galloped forward into the mass of horses streaming down the drive.

She rode packed in by strange horses, all urgently straining forward, like the Charge of the Light Brigade, Jacky thought. She grinned as she rode, loving the feeling of excitement, of really being alive. Once she glanced behind her but couldn't see Erica or Firebird. There was nothing Jacky could do about it. She couldn't stop now.

They turned into the road and, with a swell of hoofs on tarmac, cantered down it, past cars and foot followers. As they reached the end of the road the riders in front of Jacky seemed to be slowing down. Jacky stood up in her stirrups and saw that they were jumping off the road over a hunt gate. The approach to the jump was crowded with refusing hunters, riders circling their horses for a second attempt and blocking the way for the others. A competent-looking woman on a bay horse rode straight at the jump shouting to the refusers to make way there. Jacky felt Flicka chugging impatiently at the bit and, before she had time to realize what was happening, Flicka had tucked herself in at the heels of the bay. She took the hunt gate at a trot, jumping from the road and sailing over effortlessly. The woman on the bay shouted something to Jacky but Jacky couldn't hear, for the second Flicka landed she was galloping off in pursuit of the hunt.

They rode over muddy tracks through a wood. When Jacky came out of the wood she saw that the horses and riders were waiting together in a group. In front of them she saw the dappled shapes of hounds leaping like roe deer through the undergrowth of a small copse as they quartered to and fro trying to raise a fox.

Jacky pulled Flicka in at the back of the riders but despite Jacky's efforts to keep her pony still, Flicka edged and fretted her way forward.

"Can't you control that animal?" demanded a blue-cheeked woman in a high, nervous voice.

"Stand still at covert side," growled a deep-voiced man in a top hat.

"Take the blighter home if you can't ride it," snarled a man whose horse had just lashed out at Flicka.

Jacky pretended not to hear. She could see herself being carried right into the middle of hounds when, to her relief, she saw Roderick on Midas and managed to take Flicka over to him without causing too much disturbance. From the look on Roderick's face Jacky felt that he wasn't all that pleased to see her.

"Where's Erica?" he hissed.

"I don't know," admitted Jacky.

"Wheesht," commanded one of the side saddle ladies, reprimanding them for talking at covert side.

Now that Flicka had found Midas, Jacky managed to

keep her still but she knew from the pony's tense alertness that the second the hunt moved on Flicka would be galloping with them.

The encouragement of the huntsman changed to a different note. He called hounds out of a blank covert and led the field back through the wood, down a lane where the riders waited while the huntsman put hounds into a patch of gorse.

Despite Jacky's efforts to keep her back, Flicka had managed to push her way forward to the very front of the hunt. "I shouldn't be here. I know I shouldn't," Jacky thought, feeling her pony quivering with anticipation of the gallop to come. In front of her were only the Master and his wife and two or three superior, hunting types on blood hunters. There wasn't room in the lane to turn Flicka and Jacky was certain that once they all started galloping after hounds she would never be able to stop her pony. She looked back in a sudden panic trying to see Midas and Roderick but the riders waiting behind her were all strangers. Jacky felt completely alone.

Suddenly the sound of the hounds changed, there was a red flash of lithe animal as the fox broke cover on the far side of the gorse, the clear high note of the huntsman's horn and hounds poured out of the covert and streamed after the fox. Huntsman and hunt servants galloped after them, while the Master held his field in check for a minute longer, then they too were galloping over the moor. In front of them a stone wall fanned the riders out as each rider chose his own place to jump it. With all her strength Jacky struggled to control Flicka. She pulled on the snaffle bit as hard as she could, tugging with all the power in her arms to slow down her pony's mad, drumming speed. But it had no effect whatsoever. Over the wall Flicka went in a high wide arc that brought her on landing to the side of a young man on a grey. Racing shoulder to shoulder Flicka paced the grey downhill. Over another wall they went, jumping it side by side. Jacky felt Flicka's hoofs clatter on fallen stones on the far side of the wall, but, without hesitating, Flicka galloped on.

"I can't stop her," Jacky thought wildly. "I can't stop."

She braced her feet against her stirrups and pulled back on her reins. "Stop, Flicka," she cried. "Stop!"

But it was useless. She might as well have been pulling against a tank.

"Look out for the ditch on the other side," the young man shouted as they rode at a wall together.

Jacky's mouth was too dry to allow her to answer. She felt Flicka surge over the wall, see the ditch and stretch herself in mid-air to clear it. But the grey's hind legs landed in the soft banking of the ditch, she heard the young man shout, was aware that his horse was coming down before Flicka carried her relentlessly on.

There were only about half a dozen riders in front of Jacky now and a little way in front of them hounds moved in a pack, running so close together that they looked like one creature moving like quicksilver over the ground.

Two more walls, a hunt gate with the bar still on top, another wall and then hounds checked. They had lost the scent that had held them together and they split up now into separate dogs searching this way and that.

Flicka stopped with the other horses, she was gasping for breath and her coat was curded with sweat. Jacky felt the other riders, all men and women on fit hunters, looking down at her curiously, some smiling to see a pony at the front of the hunt, others irritated that a thirteen hand, trace-clipped pony should have galloped and jumped as well as their expensive horses. Jacky was too tired to care. Her arms felt like limp string, her hands that had been holding on so tightly to Flicka's reins seemed suddenly to have stopped working, she couldn't open or close them and her knees were shaking against the saddle. She looked round desperately for Roderick.

"I've got to take Flicka away," she thought. "If they start running again I'll never keep her back, never." But not one of the seven or eight riders grouped around the Master was Roderick. Jacky hadn't seen any of them in her life before. She felt tears mist her eyes. She just didn't know how to take Flicka away. Should she just turn and ride away without saying anything? Were you allowed to do that? And even if you were, Jacky wasn't too sure that she would manage to get Flicka away from hounds. "Oh, don't be so feeble," she told herself furiously.

Suddenly a hound spoke, "Hark to Dauner," cried the huntsman. "Hark to Dauner."

Jacky felt Flicka tense beneath her as other hounds found the scent again. Like bees they swarmed together and were away.

Hunters plunged and bucked to follow them.

"Give them a chance. Hold back," cried the huntsman.

In minutes it had started again but now Flicka was galloping neck for neck with the Master.

"Get that pony back," he yelled at Jacky. "Get back there."

But Jacky had no strength left to try to fight Flicka. She managed to pull her to one side of the Master's bay before they jumped a ditch but she was powerless to hold her back.

Over a low stone wall they went and as they landed Flicka was in front of the Master. Then it happened. "Oh no!" Jacky thought. "Oh please, no!" and the next minute Flicka was galloping into hounds. They broke up in confusion, one big brown dog yelping wildly as Flicka charged through them.

Some of the words the Master used when he told Jacky to take Flicka home were new to her, or, if she'd heard them before, she'd only heard them on television.

Feeling as if she would die of shame, Jacky forced Flicka away from hounds and hunters, the pony crabbed and jibbed. For a second as the hunt rode away Jacky thought Flicka was going to manage to carry her back to them. She

D

flung herself to the ground and clung on to Flicka's reins until the last horse had disappeared from sight.

Left alone the pony shrank back into her usual size. She looked thoroughly wretched. Jacky sat down on a boulder and felt sick.

Stray members of the hunt rode past and Jacky pointed out the way the hunt had gone and then one of them was Roderick.

"Did you come off?" he asked. "Flicka's in a muck sweat."

He dismounted and stood uneasily by Jacky, wondering if she was concussed and feeling guilty that she had been left alone.

"Never again," said Jacky after she had related her disastrous morning to Roderick. "Never again. Flicka's going to be a show jumper—not a hunter. I've made up my mind."

CHAPTER SEVENTEEN

"Well I warned you," Erica said when she heard about Jacky's dismal disgrace on the hunting field. "I told you it wasn't like Pony Club things."

And Celia Grunter sang, "A-Hunting We Will Go," every time she saw Jacky.

"I don't know how I'm going to survive this winter," Jacky confided to her mother. "I am in the valley of despair."

"Are you dear?" said Mrs Munro brightly.

"Yes I am. Only riding at weekends and then only hacking. Erica says we won't be able to use the paddock until the spring. Three whole months before I can start schooling Flicka again. January, February, March. Goodness knows what she'll be like by then. She was mucking about like anything on the road the other day. Ever since we went hunting she's done nothing but pull, pull, pull," and Jacky swung away irritably to wander through the house and think how unfair it all was.

Now that the ponies were in at nights, Jacky always cycled home with Erica to muck out Flicka's box, put down her bed for the night and put in her feed, hay and water.

"It's hard labour, that's all it is," said Erica, forking straw for Firebird's bed.

"I wouldn't mind if we could only ride," said Jacky, putting down a full water bucket. She loved seeing Flicka settled for the night, standing warm and cosy in deep yellow straw, her head buried in the trough as she crunched oats and chop and nuts.

Jacky never stopped being thankful for all the Dawsons had done for her and often she would imagine how difficult it would have been trying to keep Flicka in the garage patch during the long winter. All the time Jacky knew that she should have been getting on with schooling and jumping Flicka. But every weekend was either wet and the ground too soft for jumping, or frosty and the ground too hard. On the few days when Jacky did manage to persuade Erica to let her ride in the paddock, Flicka pulled like a train and at the sight of a jump she became so excited that Jacky could hardly hold her. She would gallop round and round, taking great leaps over Erica's poles and cans, while Jacky hauled helplessly on her reins.

"She's fresh," Jacky would think, trying to make excuses. "She's young and she's never been in at nights before. She's never forgotten that hunt."

But when she was being honest with herself Jacky knew that something had gone very wrong. She knew that she shouldn't pull at Flicka's mouth the way she was doing, but when Flicka was galloping madly round the jumps for the third or fourth time, Jacky couldn't think of anything else to do except to pull even harder on the reins. Flicka in her turn pulled more than ever and their jumping usually ended in a fight to see who was the strongest—a fight that Flicka always won.

"You're making her worse," said Erica. "And if you don't stop churning up that paddock it will be so rutted and dusty in the summer we won't be able to use it then either."

Jacky went home to read instructional books on riding and have nightmares about Flicka, head tossing, tail switching as she charged like a guided missile at unending jumps.

It snowed heavily in the middle of February and Mrs Dawson made Erica stack her tin cans, boxes and poles under cover.

"If you'd left them in the field we could have jumped in the snow," moaned Jacky.

"It rots them," said Erica. "We wouldn't have had any left by the spring."

The spring took a long time to come. The snow lay like a white blanket that nothing could melt. Miss Hope wrote a nasty letter to Jacky's father saying that she wasn't paying attention in class. And Jacky spent most of her time worrying about Flicka's jumping.

In April the snow vanished overnight, trees inched into green and Mrs Marshall sent Jacky a letter.

Dear Jacky,
    We are having a first try-out of the "possibles" for this year's Pony Club Team for the Inter Branch Comp. on Saturday 22nd at 10.00 a.m. at my house. Nothing too difficult. I don't expect fit ponies yet. Just one or two jumps. I want to get the team fixed up as soon as poss. so we can all train together. Hope to see you Sat.
                                        Yours sincerely,
                                        Helen Marshall.

"Goodness Jacky, what's wrong?" demanded Mrs Munro as her daughter's cry of dismay echoed round the dining-room.

"But surely that is what you were so pleased about last summer," said her mother after Jacky had explained.

"Oh, you don't understand, Mummy. That was last summer when Flicka was jumping well and everything was different. I didn't think she'd be picking the team for ages yet."

"Doesn't leave you much time to get things organized," her father said. "This Saturday she wants to see you."

"I know! Not tomorrow but the next day!"

"You'll need to work hard tomorrow evening," Mrs Munro said consolingly. But on Friday Miss Hope kept Jacky in after school because she had caught her reading

School for Young Riders under the desk, and in the end Jacky only had time for about an hour's schooling over Erica's jumps.

"Cor!" exclaimed Erica after Flicka had soared over the jumps like a whirlwind and twice round the field before Jacky could even bring her to a trot. "Honestly, I don't think Mrs Marshall will be very pleased if she behaves like that."

"I wish you were coming."

"So do I. Mrs Marshall asked me when she met me a week or two ago, but I said I was more interested in just dressage and I explained about Firebird's leg, and now Mummy's gone and made an appointment for me at the dentist."

"All the same, I do wish you were coming," Jacky said again.

She wished it even more the next morning when she rode Flicka into Mrs Marshall's field and saw Celia sitting astride a new chestnut pony.

"Don't tell me you've had the cheek to bring that creature," Celia shouted in a loud mocking voice, so that the six other Pony Club members who were considered "possibles" turned round and stared at Flicka.

"Why shouldn't she?" asked Dorothy Sloan. "It is Mrs Marshall, not you or your mother who chooses the team."

"I'd have had more sense than to ask someone who can't even control their pony."

"At least I don't cast off ponies as if they were old shoes," stated Jacky.

"I suppose you mean Prince. Goodness he was such a slug. Calypso is a million times better."

"Prince was a super pony until you ruined him," said Arthur Paterson, a boy who came from the other side of Tarentshire and rode a dun cob.

Celia ignored him. "Anyway," she said, "I expect I'll be jumping Calypso at the Horse of the Year Show. That's why Daddy bought him for me."

Before anyone had time to ask Celia what she meant, Mrs Marshall left the group of parents she had been talking to and came over to explain what she wanted them to do.

"I've decided to choose the team much earlier this year and then we can really get going and train as a team. Now, first I want to see you going over the show jumps at the other end of the field and then I've got a little course laid out with six cross-country jumps. Ride your ponies in for a minute and when you feel they're ready, come down to the jumps and we'll get started."

"It's now that everything begins to go wrong," Jacky thought as she tried to circle Flicka at a collected canter but only managed to stop her bursting into a tearaway gallop by yanking at the reins. "Oh, behave yourself, Flicka. They're only tiny jumps. Nothing to get so excited about."

As she waited for her turn to jump she felt as if she were sitting on a keg of gunpowder that might explode at any minute.

"You next," Mrs Marshall said, smiling at Jacky. "Take your time now," but before she had finished speaking Flicka had bounded past her.

In a thundering of hoofs and a rushing of cold air Jacky was carried over the jumps. Flicka was going so fast that she could hardly tell when they were actually jumping or when they were galloping in great, leaping bounds.

By pulling one rein with both hands Jacky just managed to turn Flicka and steer her over the rest of the jumps. She cleared them all effortlessly but they had almost reached the far end of the field before Jacky regained control.

By the time they had joined the others again Mrs Marshall had taken everyone across to the start of the cross country.

"Eight jumps," she was saying. "Over the log, in and out the chicken coops, downhill and over the water jump, those two walls between the flags, back over the stile and finish up over the log in the opposite direction."

Turning, she saw that Jacky had returned. "Did you get carted?" she asked her, laughing at Flicka. "She does hot up, doesn't she? Perhaps you might be safer not to try the cross country?"

"What is that ridiculous child doing now?" Mrs Grunter, who was standing watching with two other doting mothers, spoke in a voice loud enough for everyone to hear. "When she rode those old crocks she wouldn't jump and now she has a pony that will jump she's afraid of it!"

"Of course I'll try," said Jacky instantly. "Could I go first, please? Waiting makes her more excited than ever."

"Try to steady her before she gets away from you," advised Mrs Marshall, nodding.

"Okay," said Jacky as Flicka battered down the field and soared over the log with feet to spare. She flung herself at the chicken coops, clearing what was meant to be an in and out with one huge leap.

"Steady, steady," muttered Jacky, fighting to pull Flicka's head up, pulling desperately on her reins to try to slow her uncontrollable speed.

But on the slope leading down to the water jump she had no hope of slowing Flicka down. Jacky could do nothing. She had no strength left to pull any harder. She could only grip the saddle tighter between her knees and brace her feet against the stirrups as the black pony careered wildly down towards the water jump.

A split second before it happened, Jacky knew that Flicka was coming down. She felt her stumble in the soft ground, felt her struggle to stay upright, but she was going too fast to save herself.

Suddenly Jacky was flying through the air and, during that second, she caught a glimpse of Flicka turning a complete somersault.

After that everything was muddled. There were the terrible moments when Flicka lay struggling on the ground and the relief when she surged to her feet and cantered back to the other ponies, unhurt. There was picking herself up and telling everyone who had come crowding round that she was quite all right, that she really was all right. Then there was leading Flicka back to Erica's, ignoring people who stared rudely at their mud-spattered state, and there was trying not to think about how pleased Celia and Mrs Grunter would be.

Jacky led Flicka into her box, stripped off her muddy tack and fetching a curry comb and dandy brush tried to clean her pony. But the mud was too wet to brush off and the more Jacky groomed the more it clung stickily to Flicka's sides.

At last Jacky could bear it no longer. Standing staring at her filthy pony she let the tears run down her cheeks. All the hopes she had built around Flicka had all crumbled into nothing. She, Jacky Munro, had ruined a young pony. She had a pony that could jump brilliantly but she had turned her into a useless runaway. Jacky's tears left two white streaks down her muddy face.

"I'm sorry, Flicka. I didn't mean to ruin you," and she threw her arms round her pony's neck and sobbed into her mane.

Roderick, who had been schooling Midas in the paddock, rode through the yard, meaning to exercise for an hour on the roads. He heard the sound of crying and jumped off Midas to investigate. He led Midas across to Flicka's box and stood for a minute wondering if Jacky had hurt herself, but it didn't look that sort of crying to him.

"Something wrong?" he asked.

CHAPTER EIGHTEEN

Gulping, Jacky explained.

"Tough luck," Roderick said after he had listened carefully.

"And she is such a terrific jumper," said Jacky miserably.

"You can say that again. I've never seen a pony jump like her. I'll never forget the way she cleared the brush at that Pony Club thing."

"But it's no good if she runs away all the time!"

Roderick stood leaning on the half-door of the box staring at Flicka. Suddenly he spoke.

"Do you really care about Flicka's jumping?"

"What do you mean? Of course I care."

"Would you really work to try and improve her?"

"I'd do anything, honestly!"

"How would it be if you come up in the morning and I'd see if I could help you?"

"Before school?"

"Be ready to start at seven and I'm warning you to be on time. I'm not always in the best of tempers so early in the morning."

Before Jacky could thank him or ask any more questions Roderick had swung himself up on to Midas and ridden out of the yard.

When Erica heard about her brother's offer to coach Flicka and Jacky she was amazed.

"You're honoured!" she exclaimed. "It's a lot more than he would do for me and he's jolly good, even if he is my brother. He must think Flicka has tremendous promise if he's going to get up before seven to take you!"

As seven o'clock chimed from the church clock the next morning Jacky was riding Flicka round the field while Roderick sat on a tin can giving instructions.

"Now take her over the jumps," he said after Jacky had walked, trotted and cantered round the field in both directions.

Jacky turned Flicka towards the first jump and felt her pony light up beneath her; felt the wild plunge and then the thundering speed as Flicka stormed round the jumps. Furiously Jacky heaved at the reins, but for all the attention Flicka paid there might as well have been no bit in her mouth. After she had cleared all the jumps, Flicka charged round the field several times before Jacky regained control.

"That's what she's like every time we jump," Jacky said riding over to Roderick.

"Quite a whirlwind," agreed Roderick thoughtfully. "Yet it doesn't make any difference to her jumping. She never hits anything. Do you need to tug at her mouth all the time? You've only started hanging on to her reins like that since she ran away with you out hunting. That's why you got on so well with her before. You didn't interfere. I think she likes to go fast, knows she can jump best at that speed and gets mad with you for asking her to jump and then trying to stop her when she knows she's doing her best."

"But I've got to stop her somehow."

"Are you scared?"

"No! Course not. I love jumping but I hate being carted round as if I couldn't ride."

"This time," instructed Roderick, "put a knot in your reins and go round the jumps with the lightest possible touch. Only use them to guide her round at the turn. When you want her to stop, give and take on the bit. Don't hang on all the time with a dead stranglehold as if it was a tug of war."

Jacky did as she was told and jumped again, using her legs and seat to guide her pony rather than the reins. Even when she felt that Flicka was going too fast she didn't pull on the reins to try to stop her. It wasn't until Flicka had cleared the last jump that she began to steady her. But she didn't pull with a dead hold. Instead she did as Roderick had suggested, pulling and releasing the reins several times.

"Did you see her?" Jacky shouted triumphantly, clapping Flicka's sleek neck as she rode back to Roderick. "She hardly pulled at all! I was in control again almost at once!"

"That's because you were saying one definite thing. Before, you were nagging all the time but really saying nothing."

"I suppose that's right," agreed Jacky, laughing.

"You asked her to jump and then when she did what you'd told her to do you immediately started tugging madly at her mouth to try and stop her. Try her round again."

Jacky jumped round once more and rode back to Roderick beaming all over her face.

"There you are," he said. "It worked again. It isn't magic. Just horse sense. Now for the next week I want you to go on schooling her, thinking about keeping you hands as light as possible, particularly when she's jumping."

"Right," said Jacky. "The same time tomorrow morning?"

"For you and Flicka, yes. For me, no. I shall only appear unexpectedly once or twice a week. Unfortunately the university controls some of my time!"

"But I can ask you if things start going wrong again?"

"Any urgent message left for me with my mother or sister will receive immediate attention."

But things didn't go wrong. Now that Jacky had stopped pulling at Flicka's reins the pony stopped fighting her and, allowed to go at her own speed, she cleared the jumps calmly and effortlessly.

"Try her over something a bit bigger," Roderick said one morning about a month later, and they built up two of the jumps to over four feet with a big spread on them.

"Just watch her. Probably this will be the highest she's ever jumped."

But Flicka cantered serenely over them with a bright alert expression on her face that seemed to say, "This is what I call jumping."

That evening Jacky and Erica built a really big course and Jacky rode Flicka over it.

"Absolutely fabulous!" Erica exclaimed. "She didn't touch a thing. Gosh, I bet you even Midas would have a job getting round those."

"She jumps better when the jumps are higher," Jacky said, making much of Flicka. "She was really *thinking* about her jumping there."

Later on when they were cleaning tack, Roderick came into the tack room with a sheaf of papers in his hand.

"I've got the entry forms for the Royal Peterbourne Show," he said. "Would either of you like to go?"

"It would be fun," Erica said. "Though Firebird wouldn't stand much of a chance. They'd be bound to spot her leg."

"What about you, Jacky?"

Jacky stood open-mouthed, clutching a soapy tack sponge in her hand.

"You don't mean it?" she said at last. "Jump Flicka at the Peterbourne Show? But it's a huge posh show. I couldn't possibly. We're not good enough!"

"In other words you'd like to come?" laughed Rod.

"Oh, but I couldn't, not after we made such a mess at Mrs Marshall's."

"That is behind you. The Peterbourne Show is ahead. Mind you, don't think you're certain to win. The competition is pretty stiff. But it's always a good show."

"How are we getting there?" asked Erica.

"Jack Tosh wants to take his hunter to show and I thought I'd have a bash at the Working Hunter on Midas. If you two come his father says we can take their big float which holds four horses and share the price of the petrol."

"You do choose your friends well," teased Erica.

"Jacky, you'll need to register Flicka and join the B.S.J.A." Roderick said, ignoring his sister. "I'll see about it for you and make out the entries."

"Do you *really* think I should?" repeated Jacky. "I mean, honestly, I don't think it is my sort of show. Don't you think I'd be better to wait for the Pony Club gymkhana?"

"Listen to me," growled Roderick. "Flicka could go right to the top if you'll let her, or she can stay right here in Tarent, winning rosettes in Pony Club things. She's your pony. Now make up your mind once and for all."

Jacky grinned, "The top," she said.

"Good. You've got a month to practise in before Peterbourne."

CHAPTER NINETEEN

Jack Tosh, his hunter and his father's float, were all late.
Roderick had phoned the house to see if they had left but
he couldn't get any reply. Now Jacky, Erica and Roderick
were all standing in the Dawsons' yard waiting impatiently.
Roderick and Erica were both wearing black jackets, boots
and white stocks while Jacky was feeling stiffly uncomfort-
able in jodhpurs which had shrunk at the cleaners and a
tweed jacket that was really too tight to button.

"Here he is at last!" Roderick yelled as he heard the
powerful engine of the float grind up the drive.

"Battery was flat. Couldn't get her started," shouted
Jack Tosh, jumping down and hurrying round to help
Roderick lower the ramp. "Sorry about it. Who's the kid
that's jumping? Better load her pony last. We're going to
have a tight squeeze to make it in time for her. Her class is
first."

Roderick loaded Midas and tied him head to tail with a
slat separating him from Jack Tosh's big brown mare,
The Bromidge.

"We don't need to separate the others, they know each
other," Roderick said as Erica led Firebird up the ramp.
Inside the dark float, Firebird gleamed like a golden pony
with her plaited mane and oiled hoofs. Flicka too was
glossy with white light flickering on her jet black coat as
she moved.

Soon the float was swaying and rumbling on its way to
Peterbourne. Jack Tosh stepped down hard on the ac-
celerator and swung round corners on two wheels.

They arrived at the showground ten minutes before

Jacky's class was due to begin. Quickly, Jacky saddled Flicka up, mounted and began to ride Flicka about to accustom her to the strange surroundings.

"I knew I shouldn't have come," Jacky thought, staring round at the sleek blood ponies and their professional riders. "They're all sure to be far, far better than us," and she felt her stomach cold like a hard stone and her hands sticky with excitement.

"Here's your number," said Roderick. "Keep still and I'll tie it on to your back. Forty-three. Very, very lucky! Now find a decent space and get her going a bit. And stop worrying. Think about Flicka."

Jacky found a space and began to school Flicka. Once she began to concentrate on Flicka she felt a bit better, and by the time Rod called her to go into the collecting ring, she was almost feeling like herself again.

"It's a pretty stiff course," Roderick said. "Straight down the middle to start with. Then diagonally across, over the brick wall and the hog's back. Down the far side over the treble and round over the single pole and back up the middle again."

As Roderick spoke, Jacky followed the course over the jumps in the ring. "She's never tackled a treble at that height before," Jacky said, frowning.

"What's height to Flicka? Don't you interfere and she'll make it. That's the first one in now."

"That's Jane Dallas!" gasped Jacky as a girl on a dappled grey cantered round before she started jumping. "She is just about the top junior show jumper in Britain!"

"Little does she know that her position is about to be challenged!" laughed Roderick.

Jane Dallas had three refusals at the treble and rode out disqualified. Five more ponies jumped before it was Jacky's turn and out of the five only a boy on a roan pony called Romany Sixpence was clear.

"Good luck," Erica shouted as Jacky trotted Flicka into the ring.

112

"Go it, lass," cheered Jack Tosh. Then, turning to Roderick, he said, "Hard lines she has to jump in this class. Her pony can't be more than an inch over the thirteen two?"

"No, she's half an inch under it even with her shoes on," explained Erica, not taking her eyes off Jacky.

"Rubbish, Flicka is over thirteen two," exclaimed Roderick indignantly.

"Miss Hewitt let us all measure our ponies one day at a rally and Flicka is thirteen one. Definitely!" stated Erica.

"Goodness, no!" exclaimed Roderick. "But I asked Jacky when I was registering Flicka for her and I was sure she said Flicka was thirteen three hands high!"

"Well you were wrong," said Erica, and the whistle blew for Jacky to start jumping before anyone had time to say any more.

Jacky had never jumped in such a big arena in her life. She felt tiny and lost; surrounded by strangers who were sure to be criticizing her riding, her scuffed jodh. boots and her too tight jacket. "Say I burst a button just as I'm going over a jump," she thought, and giggled. The bell went and when she rode Flicka at the first jump she had stopped worrying and was only thinking how glorious it was to be Jacky Munro, really show jumping at last.

Easily Flicka cleared the parallel poles and the gate as she galloped down the centre of the ring. Then across the ring and over the big red and white wall. Six strides to the hog's back where Flicka checked before she shot into the air, realizing, just in time, how big a spread had to be cleared.

"They're huge jumps," Jacky thought, grinning. "We're really jumping. She sails over them as if she had wings!" And if she had been in Erica's field she would have shouted aloud for joy.

Now the treble lay ahead. Jacky took Flicka to the farthest corner of the ring to give her the longest possible run-in to the jumps. Flicka pranced, irritated at being checked.

"Leave her alone, leave her alone," muttered Roderick at the ringside.

Shooting forward, Flicka bounded down the side of the ring over the first part of the treble. She took a long stretching stride and then up and over the second part. As she rose over the second part, Jacky felt her pony goggle with surprise, and saw her ears prick sharply forward in amazement at another jump so soon.

"Go on," whispered Jacky, urging Flicka on with her seat. "Don't stop! Don't stop!"

"She's going to stop," groaned Erica, digging her nails into the wooden rail at the ringside.

But Flicka didn't stop. Expecting the jump to be a double, she was going too fast to put in a stride between the second and third parts of the treble. Her speed only allowed her to touch down and rise again to fly the third part of the treble. Jacky heard the early morning scatter of spectators gasp, and jack-knifed to stay with Flicka, letting the reins slip through her fingers. With a great, straining leap Flicka was over it, but, as they galloped on to the next jump, there was a crash behind them as the top bar of the third part of the treble crashed to the ground.

Flicka cleared the single pole, jumped back over the gate and the parallel poles and cantered out through the finish.

Back with Roderick, Erica and Jack Tosh, Jacky felt suddenly shy. She fussed about Flicka, loosening her girths and patting her, while the others praised Flicka's jumping, Jacky's riding and told her excitedly that even with four faults she was still second.

Ten other ponies jumped but there were no more clear rounds. A boy and a girl had four faults each.

"That means the roan pony is first and you three jump off," Roderick said.

Jacky nodded, thinking how super it was that she was going to have another chance to go round the jumps.

This time, smoothly, and loving every minute of it, Flicka jumped clear. The girl had two refusals and the boy a brick out of the wall.

A large, floral-clad woman handed the boy on the roan a silver cup and a photographer clicked his camera. Then the woman pinned the blue rosette on to Flicka's bridle.

"You've got a game little pony there," she said, rubbing Flicka's neck. "Well done, very well done indeed. There's nothing I like better than to see a little'un having a shot over the big course."

Jacky nodded and grinned and said thank you. Even now the jumping was over, the jumps still seemed huge and, really, the other prize-winning ponies were all bigger than Flicka. At Pony Club rallies the ponies in A and B rides always jumped together so that Jacky was quite used to jumping against bigger ponies and hadn't really noticed it until now.

"It's strange at a big show like this," Jacky thought as she cantered round, "having different sized ponies jumping together." But she was too overjoyed that Flicka had jumped so well to be really worried about it.

Jacky rode out of the ring and looked for Roderick and the others, thinking that they might have gone back to the box and be unloading their mounts. Then she spotted them still leaning against the rail at the ringside and roaring with laughter. Jacky rode across wondering what could be so funny.

"If you could have seen her," laughed Erica. "Bouncing along behind Romany Sixpence as cheeky as could be!"

"I was just thinking how big the other ponies were. I thought Flicka would have been about the biggest in her class."

"Listen," said Roderick. "Listen carefully and accept my humble apologies. I thought Flicka was over thirteen

115

two. That was the fourteen two and under championship that you have just jumped in."

"What?" cried Jacky.

"And," continued Roderick, "since you were second and since this is the Royal Peterbourne Show, you are now qualified to enter for the Junior Show Jumper of the Year at Wembley next October!"

CHAPTER TWENTY

Never before had Jacky known time drag so slowly as it did between the Peterbourne Show in June and the Horse of the Year Show in October.

For the first week after Peterbourne Jacky couldn't believe that it was true. She would wake up in the morning and lie for a second warm and cosy, then suddenly remember and shiver with excitement. It was really true, she *was* going to jump Flicka at Wembley in the Leading Junior Show Jumper of the Year Championship!

Roderick wrote away for the entry forms and received a complicated booklet full of rules and regulations and forms to fill in if you wanted stabling overnight.

"Gosh," exclaimed Jacky. "I could never sort it out myself."

"Not to worry. You have your manager here," said Roderick in a pompous voice. "I think I might take Midas too, just for a laugh. If I can talk Jack Tosh into having a bash at the Working Hunter with me we could take his old man's float. That would save us a lot of bother. We shall all have a fantastic week at Wembley. Erica, you shall come as groom."

Erica grinned.

"Don't you wish you were riding?" Jacky asked her.

"No point," said Erica. "They wouldn't look at Firebird because of her leg. And I'd much rather wait now and get a really good young horse to school for dressage competitions. Anyway, I wouldn't dream of selling Firebird."

Jacky took Flicka to four other shows throughout the summer and jumped her in the 14.2 classes. They were first twice, second once and unplaced once, on a day of wind and rain that terrified Flicka.

Jacky was careful not to overjump her pony in case she sickened her. She spent more time working at her dressage with Erica or hacking Flicka along the roads, to make sure that she was really fit, than she did jumping. But one evening, Roderick, Jack Tosh and Jacky took their horses by float to a riding school that boasted a big indoor school. Here they jumped under the strange conditions of artificial light. At first Flicka spooked and shied but soon she settled down. The other two didn't take any notice of the lights at all.

Mr and Mrs Munro were thrilled at their daughter's success but it didn't stop Mr Munro asking about Jacky's homework.

"But Daddy, I can't do homework in the summer holidays," Jacky cried.

"Mr Knowles's daughter does a little arithmetic and a little English right through the holidays."

"Oh, but look at her! You wouldn't like me to become like that?"

Mr Munro laughed at his daughter's disgust.

Jacky and her mother went into Tarent and bought new jodhpurs and a new riding jacket.

"They nearly drown me," Jacky said as she showed them to Erica that evening. "Mummy wouldn't buy them any smaller. She said I'd grow into them!"

"So you will," giggled Erica. "In about ten years time. I saw Celia today and she's got new stretch ones. She still says she's going to Wembley but I'm sure she hasn't qualified Calypso. They took him to Burghley for the Championship as a last hope. But they weren't placed. I looked up the results in *Horse and Hound*."

"Now that she can't be nasty about Flicka, she just ignores me. I hope she doesn't go. It would spoil everything to have her fat face smirking there," said Jacky with feeling.

118

That evening, Mr Grunter came to see Mr Munro and offered to buy Flicka for eight hundred pounds.

"Nothing to do with me," said Mr Munro, his face serious but his eyes twinkling. "You'll need to ask Jacky. Flicka belongs to her."

"If you were to offer three thousand I wouldn't sell her," Jacky muttered furiously.

And Mr Munro showed Mr Grunter out.

"So that's what they're trying to do now," said Roderick when Jacky told him. "Going to buy a pony that someone else has qualified."

"We'll need to set a guard over Flicka," said Erica. "Those Grunters would stop at nothing."

"You can laugh," Jacky said to Roderick, "but you don't know them the way we do."

Then at last it was October. The Horse of the Year Show started on Tuesday the 2nd. They were taking the horses up in Jack Tosh's float on Thursday morning and staying until Saturday night.

"Just in case we're needed for the Grand Parade," joked Roderick.

Now that the show was so close, Jacky never thought of anything else from the minute she opened her eyes in the morning until she shut them at night. At school she made little lists and passed them to Erica under the desk.

"Jumping studs; Bandages; Rugs," wrote Jacky.

"Put your pencil down," screamed Miss Hope. "I am really annoyed with you, Jacqueline Munro."

Jacky sighed and thought for the hundredth time how awful it would be if she took the wrong course and ruined Flicka's chances.

On Wednesday night both Jack Tosh and Jacky stayed at the Dawsons'. Everything was ready for the morning. They were leaving at five o'clock and hoped to reach London by eight; the preliminary rounds for the Leading Junior Show Jumper of the Year were at eleven-thirty in the outdoor arena.

"I shan't sleep a wink," Jacky said as she got into bed.

"Neither shall I," agreed Erica, but after they had talked for about an hour Erica was asleep.

Jacky tossed and turned, thinking about tomorrow. It was her chance to prove that Flicka really was one of the top show jumping ponies. By this time tomorrow night it would be all over. Either her dreams would all have come true or they would be in ruins.

The bright moonlight streamed in through the window and Jacky remembered the night when Flicka had jumped out of the garage patch and bolted back to the riding school.

Suddenly Jacky stopped trying to sleep. It was no good, she was too excited. She would go and see Flicka, just for a few minutes. Very quietly she got out of bed, slipped on her shoes and her anorak and crept downstairs. Quietly she closed the back door behind herself and stood gazing around at the moon-silvered silence of the night.

She walked round to the yard. "Flicka," she whispered, "Flicka." And her pony looked out over the half-door of her box, surprised to see Jacky at this time of night.

"Dear pony," Jacky murmured, running her hand down her pony's neck and gently pulling her ears. "Do your best tomorrow. Jump well."

Suddenly Jacky was sure that there was someone watching her. She felt the skin creep on her scalp and stood terrified, afraid to turn round. Flicka too pricked her ears sharply forward, watching something.

Jacky dug her nails into her palm. "Who's there?" she shouted in a trembling voice. Then, forcing herself to look round, she screamed at the top of her voice, frightening the stabled horses, waking Roderick and sending him crashing downstairs to discover what was wrong. For as Jacky had looked round, a dark shape had run swiftly from the shadow of the tack room into the shelter of the trees.

"Some gypsy or other," Roderick had said after he had

given Jacky a lecture about going out alone in the middle of the night.

But Jacky didn't think it had been a gypsy. Jacky thought it had been Celia Grunter.

CHAPTER TWENTY-ONE

"Number 125, Miss J. Munro on Flicka."

The steward's voice called Jacky from the outside collecting ring into the inside collecting ring where the next four ponies to jump waited their turn.

Jacky walked Flicka round. Her heart banged against her ribs, her stomach was a hard ball and her whole body felt cold and shivery. She had never been so nervous in all her life. Even this morning, when all the entrants for the Leading Junior Show Jumper Championship had jumped in the outdoor ring in the preliminary round, she hadn't felt nervous.

Eighteen ponies had qualified to jump in the Championship. Flicka was one of them. Now, as they waited to ride out into the brilliantly lit arena, Jacky was numb with fear. She tried to smile at Roderick and Erica who were standing at the rails but her face was too stiff.

"Smile," Jacky told herself. "Smile. Don't let Celia Grunter see you looking afraid."

For the pony to jump before Jacky was a piebald pony called Majorette. Yesterday she had belonged to Mr Brady, a horse dealer from Somerset. Today she belonged to Mr Grunter. Majorette had been qualified for Wembley by Andy, Mr Brady's son. Yesterday Andy had been expecting to jump the pony at Wembley. Today he stood watching while Celia jumped her. Majorette had jumped well enough in the preliminary to qualify her to jump in the indoor arena, but watching Majorette fight against Celia's rough riding as she trotted round the collecting ring, Andy Brady wondered how long the pony would remember his schooling, how soon she would rebel against her new rider.

So far there had been two clear rounds. To Jacky the jumps looked like huge barricades, at least ten feet high. Yet they weren't really any higher than the jumps had been that morning.

"It's being inside," Jacky thought. "It's so strange. It feels all wrong." And she clapped Flicka's neck to comfort herself with the familiar strength of her pony.

Celia and Majorette rode into the ring.

"Jolly good luck, darling," trilled Mrs Grunter.

"It's me next," Jacky thought and couldn't believe it. Everything seemed to be happening a long way off. She could only think about how cold she was and the way her knees wouldn't fit against the saddle.

"Snap out of it," Roderick growled as she rode past him. Again Jacky tried to smile but couldn't.

"Jolly good show, dear. Wonderful clear round."

Celia came charging out of the ring to her mother's praise.

Jacky shortened her reins, touched her legs to Flicka's sides and left the safety of the collecting ring to ride into the brightness of the arena.

And instantly as she rode into the light she forgot to feel afraid; forgot that she was only Jacky Munro riding a pony she had bought for three hundred pounds; forgot everything except the strength and willingness of her pony and the knowledge that they were here to jump as they had never jumped before.

Jacky cantered Flicka in a circle. The course they were to take over the jumps was crystal clear in her mind and she grinned broadly as Flicka plunged forward trying to buck.

The bell went, sharp and clear. Jacky finished the half-circle and rode through the start. Flicka pranced on the spot, the tan spurting from under her hoofs.

"On you go," murmured Jacky, easing her fingers on

the reins, and Flicka flew forward over the first jump.

As Flicka soared upwards Jacky took more weight on her stirrups and felt her stirrup leathers uneven. The right one seemed longer than the left. She remembered thinking the same thing when she had been jumping in the morning and had meant to check them but in the excitement of the moment had forgotten.

Flicka cantered on and over the brush. Round the bottom of the ring and the double was in front of them. With a long, reaching stride between the two jumps, Flicka was over, clear.

Out in the darkness beyond the brightness of the ring, Jacky could feel the crowd watching them, riding with her, catching their breath at every jump.

Over parallel poles, then over cross poles and then across the ring and over a ROAD CLOSED. Again Jacky felt her stirrups irritatingly uneven.

Round the top of the ring and down the side was the solid lane of the three jumps that formed the treble. Jacky rode confidently at it knowing that Flicka was loving the excitement, the thrill and the challenge as much as herself.

Flicka rose to the first part of the treble and, just when her riding needed all her concentration, Jacky felt again the annoying unevenness in her stirrups.

Flicka landed, took two strides, rose in a flowing arc over the second part of the treble. But this time as Jacky leant forward with her pony her right stirrup leather snapped and her stirrup fell clattering into the jump. Instantly Jacky kicked her other foot free and rode without stirrups as Flicka cleared the third part of the treble.

For a second Jacky wondered whether she should stop and wait till they found her stirrup but she knew it would take too long. She would need to ride the rest of the course without stirrups, and Jacky turned Flicka to take the last two jumps—a hog's back and the brick wall.

At the hog's back Flicka took off sooner than Jacky expected and she was badly left behind. At once she let go of the reins, knowing that Flicka would need all the luck in the world to clear the spread and a jog in the mouth could easily make her drop her hind legs into the poles. Flicka seemed to hang poised over the jump and then, with a kick back, she was over. There was no crash of falling poles but Jacky knew it must have been a very near thing.

The giant red brick wall loomed in front of them. It was too late for Jacky to try and gather up her reins. There was nothing she could do but ride Flicka on at it. Flicka jumped in a wide, smooth arc so that Jacky, riding without reins or stirrups, never moved in the saddle.

They were clear! Triumphantly, Flicka cantered through the finish. Applause burst around them as Jacky rode back to take her leather and stirrup from one of the stewards.

"Don't like the look of that one bit, me dear," the man said handing them to Jacky. "Why, you'd think someone had cut the leather on purpose."

And Jacky saw that what he said was true. Close to the buckle the leather had been cut nearly all the way across.

"Really, Jacqueline, one would have expected you to check your tack before you came here!" shouted Mrs Grunter as Jacky rode out.

Jacky looked up and saw Mrs Grunter holding Majorette and also saw Celia scuttling across the collecting ring and knew that she hadn't been mistaken. The person she had seen last night bursting out of the Dawsons' tack room to the shelter of the trees had definitely been Celia.

Roderick and Erica came rushing up and showered Flicka and Jacky with congratulations. Roderick threaded one of his leathers through Jacky's stirrup and put it on to her saddle.

"I can't imagine how that happened," he said.

But Jacky didn't explain. She didn't want a lot of fuss until she had finished jumping.

There were five clear rounds—two girls, one boy, Jacky

and Celia. They were to jump off over the same course with several of the jumps raised.

As she walked Flicka round the collecting ring, Jacky caught Celia's eye and stared hard at her. Celia turned scarlet and looked away at once.

"Nasty little beast," Jacky thought. "Little sneak."

Celia rode into the ring but this time it was obvious that something was wrong. She seemed flustered and upset. After two jumps she took the wrong course and was eliminated.

"You stupid, stupid child! Do you think your father paid all that money for you to throw away your chances by taking the wrong course?"

Mrs Grunter's furious tones echoed in Jacky's ears as she rode into the ring a second time.

Again, Flicka jumped a clear round.

The boy, Garth Ramsay, was clear as well. They would need to jump off against the clock. The boy jumped first. He did a clever round in a medium time. To win, Jacky would need to go clear and fast.

The whistle blew and Flicka galloped at the first jump, as keen and as willing to go round the course again as she had been the first time.

"Faster, faster," Jacky whispered, urging her on.

Like a whirlwind they stormed round the course. Recklessly, Jacky cut corners, let Flicka fly down the treble, come tearing up over the hog's back and shoot over the giant wall to land and beat up to the finish as if Flicka were a thoroughbred racehorse.

Applause burst and swelled over them. They were clear and with a faster time than Garth Ramsay. Flicka was the Leading Junior Show Jumper of the Year.

Jacky hardly knew what to do. She felt as if she would burst with happiness. She couldn't make enough fuss of Flicka, couldn't thank her enough and then Roderick, Erica, her parents, and Jack Tosh were crowding round, congratulating, praising, overflowing with excitement.

126